REFLECTIONS ON COMMAND:

KIT CARSON AT THE FIRST BATTLE OF ADOBE WALLS

ROY F. SULLIVAN

authorHOUSE®

AuthorHouse™
1663 Liberty Drive
Bloomington, IN 47403
www.authorhouse.com
Phone: 1 (800) 839-8640

Published by AuthorHouse   10/08/2015

ISBN: 978-1-5049-5408-2 (sc)
ISBN: 978-1-5049-5409-9 (e)

Print information available on the last page.

TABLE OF CONTENTS

LIST OF ILLUSTRATIONS

AUTHOR'S NOTE

This work is historical fiction--not pure history--since all dialogue cannot be documented, i.e., "footnoted." All other details are accurate.

Likely conversations are added to make this a lively read rather than a well-documented but sere account of this extraordinary man and commander, Colonel (later Brevet Brigadier General of Volunteers) Christopher Houston "Kit" Carson.

OTHER BOOKS BY THE AUTHOR

By Roy F. Sullivan:

Scattered Graves: The Civil War Campaigns of Confederate Brigadier
General and Cherokee Chief Stand Watie
The Civil War in Texas and the Southwest
The Texas Revolution: The Texas Navies
The Texas Revolution: Tejano Heroes
Escape from Phnom Penh: Americans in the Cambodian War
Escape from the Pentagon

By R.F. Sullivan:

A Jan Kokk Mystery: The Curacao Connection
A Jan Kokk Mystery: Murder Cruises the Antilles
A Jan Kokk Mystery: Gambol in Vegas
A Jan Kokk Mystery: Murder by the Dozen
A Jan Kokk Mystery: Crises in Kerrville

CHRISTOPHER HOUSTON (KIT) CARSON

Carson's autobiography begins simply. "I was born on December 24, 1809, in Madison County, Kentucky. My parents moved to Missouri when I was one year old and settled in what is now Howard County. For two or three years after our arrival we had to remain forted, (Note: A forted house was a stout log structure, loop-holed and barricaded against Indian attack). Also necessary were armed men stationed at the end of the fields for the protection of those that were laboring."

The first paragraph of Carson's autobiography foretells of his future hazardous life.

From childhood Carson grew up knowing about Indian dangers and appropriate safeguards. He carried those lessons throughout an active career in the mountains, deserts and plains of the "Great American West."

In August 1826 teenager Carson hired on to a party of plainsmen bound for Santa Fe. Eventually young Carson made his way to Taos, New Mexico, then a settlement. Later Taos would become the way station--later home--of his adult life.

Traveling all over the west, he worked as a driver, interpreter, hunter, trapper, teamster, tracker, dispatch rider, guide, Indian agent and Army officer. His quick abilities were as varied as his jobs. Always there was personal contact between Carson, wherever he went, with Native Americans.

Physically, Carson was small, only five feet, four inches tall, with light brown hair and grayish eyes. Although quiet, he didn't avoid violence when provoked. He took his first Indian scalp at the age of nineteen.

At one famous incident in 1835 Carson confronted and fought a large, very strong French Canadian trapper named Joseph Chouinard. This man insulted an Arapaho woman, Singing Grass--whom Carson subsequently married--as well as all the Americans in Carson's trapping party.

Carson--probably physically the smallest American in the whole group--—finally had enough when Chouinard loudly threatened to "switch" all the Americans in camp.

Carson retorted "Stop right now or else I'll rip your guts!"

The two men retrieved their weapons (Carson, a pistol, Chouinard, a rifle), mounted their horses and met in the center of the camp. Face to face, astride their mounts, more angry words and threats were exchanged. Then the antagonists both fired a single shot at the other.

Carson's round passed through Chouinard's hand and tore away a thumb. The French Canadian's bullet merely creased Carson's face, leaving a lifetime scar over his left ear.

Frightened and bleeding, the larger man begged Carson for his life and this may have ended the affair. Some say the big trapper later died of his untreated wounds. Others say Carson finished him off with a second shot.

Sadly, Carson's Arapaho wife, Singing Grass, died following the birth of their second child in 1839. Carson always extolled Singing Grass. "She was a good wife to me," he intimated to a friend.

Although illiterate, (he could scratch his name) Carson's verbal skills were superb. He spoke Spanish, Cheyenne, Arapaho, Ute, Apache, Comanche, Piaute, Shoshone, Navajo, Crow, Blackfoot and French Canadian. If the local Native American dialect was unfamiliar, he could converse fluently in sign language.

Carson spoke the clear, plain language of the western frontier, minus genteel nuances of the times.

Adventures with famous western figures became routine for Carson. Among the most famous of his friends, companions and employers were Jim Bridger, John Fremont and Stephen Kearny.

Although unknown to him at the time, Carson's fame back east was fanned by heroic pulp novels in which his derring-do was popularized.

In 1841 he married a Cheyenne woman whose name translated "Making-Out-Road." Their marriage was short-lived and she evicted Carson from her lodge after a few months of heated arguments.

The next year Carson fell in love with the beautiful fourteen-year old daughter of a prominent Taos, New Mexico family. Her name was Josefa Jaramillo and she would bear him eight children over the course of their long marriage. Carson lovingly called his wife "Chapita" while she usually referred to him more formally as "Cristobal."

Although he performed many military services throughout his life, it was not until 1847 that his military service was recognized, almost.

During an 1847 White House appointment, President James K. Polk told Carson he was being nominated for a commission as "Lieutenant of Rifles, U.S. Army." Strangely, the Senate failed to confirm his commission.

For a number of years thereafter Carson guided military campaigns against Indians committing crimes against pioneer wagon trains and settlements throughout the west.

Carson, always friendly with the Ute Indians who called him "Father Kit," became the U.S. agent to their tribe in 1854. He used his three-bedroom home in Taos as the Ute agency office. He often met, conferred with and gave food to his constituents in the front yard. Carson served in that capacity until the 1860's.

In 1861 Carson was appointed a Lieutenant Colonel commanding the First New Mexico Volunteer Infantry. He would command that and other regiments in successive campaigns at Valverde, New Mexico, (1862) and Adobe Walls, Texas, (1864).

By 1864 the being-established western frontier of the United States was in shambles. Indian attacks and deprivations terrorized thousands of settlers, many of whom hastily packed up their belongings and abandoned new homes and farms. As a result the frontier contracted eastward as far as one or two hundred miles in places. Some settlers found themselves back on the properties they had occupied years earlier.

In 1865 President Abraham Lincoln promoted Carson to the rank of Brevet Brigadier General of Volunteers. Thereafter, to his usual embarrassment, he was addressed as "General."

"Just call me Kit," he would respond.

CARSON'S NEW MISSIONS

In September 1862 Brigadier General James H. Carleton assumed command of the 9th Military Department of the Unites States which encompassed the Territory of New Mexico. Carleton was a strange mixture of martinet, perfectionist and knightly gentleman with eclectic tastes. Among his varied interests were meteorites, shipbuilding, waltzing and Russian Cossacks.

No stranger to the west or New Mexico, one of Carleton's goals in his new command was the subjugation of the Navajo tribe, the *Dine'*.

"When I came here this time," he penned, "it not only became my professional business, but my duty to residents and to the Government, to devise some plan which might, with God's blessing, forever bring these troubles to an end. These Navajo Indians…must be whipped and fear us before they will cease killing and robbing the people."

Carleton immediately selected Carson whom he had known and admired since Carleton was a Major of Dragoons twenty years earlier. The two were friends, as were their families and both belonged to the Masons.

Here was the easy solution to Carleton's "Navajo problem." Simply order reliable experienced Kit Carson to execute the General's plan to punish, relocate and subdue those belligerent, elusive Navajos.

Carson first must destroy the crops upon which the Navajos depended for life. Then forcibly march them, group by group, four hundred miles from their traditional homeland to a remote eastern area on the alkaline-rich Pecos River. The miserable area Carleton had selected for the Navajos was called the Bosque Redondo or Round Forest.

The estimated thirteen thousand Navajos endured short rations, disease, cold weather and exposure enroute to the Bosque. Once arrived they found an old enemy, the Mescalero Apaches, had been forced to precede them to the enclave. The Mescaleros provided Carleton a "dry-run" of his larger plan, the forced migration of the Navajo tribe to the same remote area.

Carleton's plan was similar to President Andrew Jackson's earlier, callous removal of the Cherokee and other tribes from the southeastern U.S. to the Indian Territory, now the State of Oklahoma.

Jackson's bestial operation began with the forced migration of the Choctaws from their homes in 1831. Later the other civilized tribes (Chickasaw, Cherokee, Seminole, and Muskogee or Creek) were forced west.

By 1837 Jackson had forced an estimated 46,000 Native Americans to move out of their southeastern lands. This allowed whites to take over Indian farms and homes and expand their fortunes at the expense of the displaced Native Americans.

The removal of the civilized tribes from the southeast was called the "Trail of Tears" due to the death of many Indians during their forced march westward. They suffered from exposure, disease, and bad rations provided by government contractors.

The forced march of the Navajos by Carleton was known simply as "The Long March." Like Jackson's earlier "Trail of Tears," it was equally hazardous and detrimental to the Navajos.

Kit Carson tried to resign his commission in February 1863. He wanted to evade Carleton's punitive plans against the Navajo and instead spend his remaining years with his growing family. A nagging chest pain, eventually diagnosed as an aortic aneurysm, reminded Carson that his time was limited.

General Carleton denied Carson's resignation and ordered him to get moving on the Navajo solution. The General's guidance to his field commander was terse. "You know where to find the Indians, you know what atrocities they have committed, you know how to punish them."

To Kit Carson an order was an order and would be obeyed whether he liked it or not. Previously, at the battle of Valverde, he had obeyed Union Colonel Edward Canby's order to withdraw from the battle despite the success of Carson's New Mexico regiment. In Carson's s sector of the Valverde battle line, his regiment was routing the Texas Confederates of General Sibley.

Carson obeyed Canby's withdrawal order, shepherding his volunteers back across a freezing Rio Grande River under enemy fire and back to Fort Craig, their starting point.

On a later, cold, snow-laden 6 January 1864 Carson led five hundred troops out of a New Mexico fort. General Carleton's orders were to invade the Navajo heartland at Canyon de Chelly, defeat any opposition, destroy Navajo crops and livestock and force march any survivors to Bosque Redondo, four hundred miles away.

The Navajo were as elusive as foxes so Carson resorted to destroying their about-to-be-harvested crops of corn, wheat and vegetables. Navajo livestock was either killed or herded away for consumption by the Army.

Carson's soldiers torched thousands of acres of crops. He estimated that nearly two million pounds of food ready for harvest had been destroyed by that October.

Without food to carry them through the harsh winter, the starving Navajo were forced out of hiding to begin a slow, tortuous march toward the Bosque Redondo.

By late February Carson was exhausted and suffering increasing pain from an old wound, having been rolled on, then dragged by his fallen horse. The Navajo "Long March" had begun and could be left for others to complete the grisly mission. Carson finally made it home to wife Josefa and children in Taos.

General Carleton had other plans for his old and famous friend. Basking in his perceived success with the "Navajo problem," Carleton turned to other headaches. This time it was the Plains Indians.

Comanche warriors and their Kiowa, Arapaho and Apache allies attacked hundreds of wagon trains arriving in New Mexico via the Santa Fe Trail and Canadian River.

No wagon trains were exempt, not even those defended by many, well-armed pioneers. Wagon trains' occupants were in constant danger of being murdered, raped, kidnapped or tortured.

Even communications between General Carleton and the War Department in Washington were jeopardized. Plains Indians were cutting transmission lines and pulling down telephone/telegraph poles.

The Washington order went out. "Punish the responsible savages." Carleton assigned yet another mission to capable, experienced Indian fighter Kit Carson.

This mission: organize a force of New Mexican and Californian Volunteers, enter the valley of the Canadian River in the Texas Panhandle where an October report indicated the hostiles were hunkered down for the winter. Punish them.

ORGANIZATION AND EQUIPMENT

Carson began assembling the various troop detachments authorized him by ambitious, micromanaging General Carleton. Carson's new command was called the 1st New Mexico Cavalry. His troops were a mixture of trained and untrained California and New Mexico Volunteers. Their assembly point was run-down old Fort Bascom, just north of the present city of Tucumcari, New Mexico, and close to the southern branch of the Canadian River.

The Canadian was a watery highway into the heart of Comancheria where large groups of Comanches and Kiowas were reported to be wintering. Their numerous villages were reported to be somewhere near the Canadian River in the Texas Panhandle.

Twenty-seven wagons of ammunition, rations for 45 days and equipment would supply Carson's command on its journey seeking combat with the elusive, powerful Plains Indian tribes. Carson was also authorized a surgeon to accompany his expedition, Doctor George S. Courtright, and an ambulance wagon.

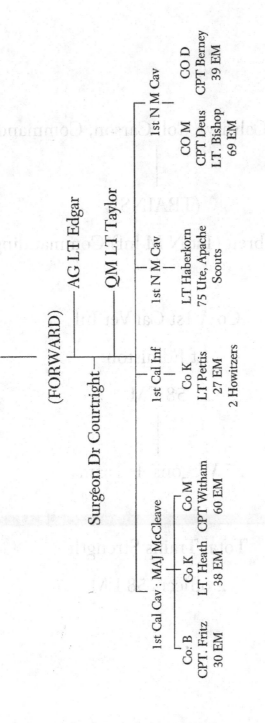

1st N M Calvary : Col. Carson, Commanding

(FORWARD)

AG LT Edgar

QM LT Taylor

Surgeon Dr Courtright

1st Cal Cav : MAJ McCleave

Co. B
CPT. Fritz
30 EM

Co K
LT. Heath
38 EM

Co M
CPT Witham
60 EM

1st Cal Inf

Co K
LT Pettis
27 EM
2 Howitzers

1st N M Cav

LT Haberkorn
75 Ute, Apache
Scouts

1st N M Cav

CO M
CPT Deus
LT. Bishop
69 EM

CO D
CPT Berney
39 EM

Total Forward Strength
12 Officers, 263 EM

1st N M Calvary : Col. Carson, Commanding

|

(TRAINS)

LTC Abreu (1st N M lnf) Commanding

|

Co A 1st Cal Vet Inf

Lt Edmiston

58 EM

|

27 Wagons + Teams

Total Trains Strength

2 officers 58 EM

The above charts outline Carson's new command either as his *forward* element to be deployed upon contact with the enemy or his trains (rear support) element.

Individual weapons of the expedition were a mixture of Sharps rifle/ carbines and Springfield rifle/muskets. The caliber.52 Sharps was the usual and better weapon carried by the California Volunteers.

The New Mexico Volunteers were equipped with either the caliber .58 or the older, less accurate caliber .69 Springfield rifle/musket.

The only crew-served weapons of Carson's expedition were two M1841 Mountain Howitzers, firing a 12-pound case, canister or explosive round. The howitzer's effective range, firing the explosive round, was about 1,000 yards. Lieutenant George H. Pettis was assigned as Carson's howitzer battery commander.

Considering his long friendship with the Utes, as well as having been their Indian agent, Carson easily recruited over seventy Mohuache Utes and a few Jicarilla Apaches as Scouts for his punitive expedition.

A friend, Cimarron rancher Lucien Maxwell, gathered his Utes with whom Carson bargained for their services as Scouts on his expedition to the Texas Panhandle.

Their pay was to be the plunder they could collect and carry home. A good string of ponies was considered a treasure for a warrior, especially were the ponies stolen from an enemy. The Utes also demanded their families be fed at the Maxwell ranch during their absence with Carson.

The supply officer at Fort Union issued Carson one hundred caliber .58 rifles as well as 120 blankets and shirts for his Indian Scouts.

Carson held a short meeting with his officers and the Ute chief. He reiterated their mission was to find and punish the Plains tribes who habitually raided and looted the wagon trains heading westward along the Santa Fe Trail.

He detailed the order of march for their departure from Fort Bascom early the next morning. Carson and the Scouts would lead, followed by half of the cavalry. Next would be the two howitzers, more cavalry, then the infantry and trains. Last in the column would be a cattle herd, extra horses and drovers.

He ordered the commanders to line up their units in order so their departure the next morning would be simple and quick.

Carson also announced his intention to personally inspect mounts, teams and wagons that evening. When his command departed Fort Bascom the next morning, it would be as combat ready as Carson could make it.

THE APPROACH MARCH

12 November 1864:

After spending several hours the night before conferring with Chief Kaniache, his lead Scout, Carson had the bugler sound reveille and his troops began assembling on their mounts and wagons after breakfast. Chief Kaniache was more than a friend. In the 1850s he had saved Carson's life when an angry Ute named Blanco pulled out a pistol, intending to shoot Carson. Kaniache knocked the pistol out of Blanco's hand.

He and Kaniache agreed that the old trails skirting the north side of the Canadian would provide the fastest, best concealed and most reliable approach once the Canadian was forded several miles below Fort Bascom.

The sole American eyewitness account of the travel to and eventual first battle of Adobe Walls was that of Lieutenant Pettis who commanded the artillery battery of twin howitzers. In his recollections of the crossing, Pettis penned, "After some difficulty in crossing the Canadian River, to the north side, the expedition was well on the war path before noon."

THE APPROACH MARCH

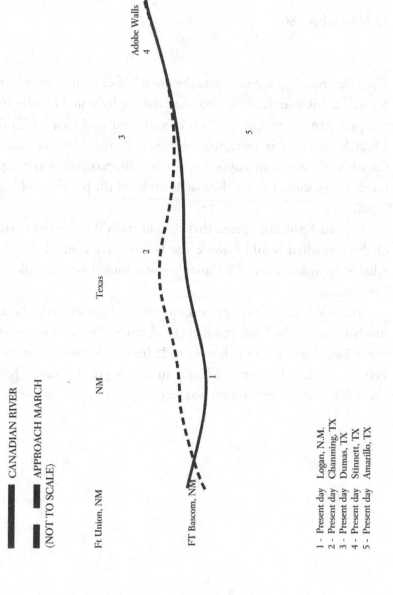

▬▬▬ CANADIAN RIVER

▬ ▬ ▬ APPROACH MARCH
(NOT TO SCALE)

Ft Union, NM   NM   Texas   Adobe Walls

FT Bascom, NM

1 - Present day   Logan, N.M.
2 - Present day   Channing, TX
3 - Present day   Dumas, TX
4 - Present day   Stinnett, TX
5 - Present day   Amarillo, TX

Despite the crossing spot's rocky bottom, fording it was as difficult for the wagon drivers as for their mules. Several wagons required minor repair before Carson's column of cavalry, artillery, infantry, trains (wagons) and livestock could be re-assembled on the north bank of the river and continue headed northeast toward Romero Draw, some four miles distant.

On arrival at the Draw, Carson and Kaniache turned onto the trail heading eastward toward Ute Creek, their first planned overnight campsite.

Joining Carson and the Scouts near the head of the column was their medical doctor, George C. Courtright, wisely attempting to escape the persistent dust raised in the rear of the column. Doctor Courtright claimed that in a lead position he could prepare a site for his field hospital before the majority of troops in the rear of the column--who might need medical attention--arrived.

By late afternoon, the entire column had descended to the first campground, Ute Springs, which lead further south to the Canadian River. Ute Springs was well chosen, offering fresh water, some forage, and concealment under the many mesquite trees lining the springs.

Mules were unhitched, cattle corralled and horses unsaddled while a few more wagons required repair. After building fires and heating rations, the troops not detailed to guard duty wrapped themselves in their blankets, anticipating sleep.

The Ute and Apache Scouts had other ideas. They kept the soldiers awake most of the night with yells and whoops, loudly brandishing weapons during an all night war dance. The dance was to be habitual until contact made with the hostiles.

13 November 1864:

Up early the next morning, troops groggily sipped scalding coffee accompanied by cold hardtack or biscuits, stowed their equipment, saddled mounts and prepared to move out.

As the previous day, the Scouts and Carson led the way, followed by Doctor Courtright and the mounted troops. Lieutenant Pettis' artillery battery of two mountain howitzers was followed by the infantry, trains (supply wagons), cattle and drovers.

The trail climbed the slope of Ute Creek to reach a flat area stretching to the east. Carson and Kaniache located a passable wagon trail roughly paralleling the north bank of the Canadian.

After several miles, the trail skirted three canyons jutting out of the Canadian valley and into another open area. Despite the flatness of this area, the earth was soft enough to make the wagons wheels sink. This caused the tired mules and drivers extra effort. Three miles later, the land became firmer and easier to traverse.

Throughout the day the Scouts patrolled the flanks as well as the front of the column, alert for hunting or war parties of the Comanche or Kiowa.

A priority for all campsites was the availability of fresh water for humans and animals. A site called Red River Springs was chosen to end the second day of the march toward the enemy winter encampments.

After several miles of gently sloping plains, another steep incline caused more difficulty for the wagons teetering down the trail toward an area of cottonwood trees, then veering sharply to the southeast before turning back eastward.

On reaching Red River Springs, the wagons were assembled on a flat area and their teams unhitched for watering. The troops quickly accustomed themselves to the new camp, realizing that each eastward mile thrust them farther into territory within easy reach of the Comanches and Kiowas.

Sentinels were posted along the perimeter, fires started and rations cooked. By dusk the Scouts returned to camp, reporting no signs of hostiles. To the groans of the troops attempting to sleep, the Scouts began their nightly war dance and chants lasting until first light.

14 November 1864:

Colonel Carson chose to spend the next day in camp, allowing the men to rest and maintain weapons and equipment. Wagons were repaired, axles greased, horses and mules re-shod as needed and coffee boiled while rations prepared.

Carson also used this time to recount to the soldiers his experiences following an 1849 attack of a group of settlers by a band of Jicarilla Apaches near their present campground.

An American named James M. White left his wagon train accompanied by his wife, Ann; daughter Virginia and five adult males. The wagon train had halted, awaiting the arrival of fresh mules from Santa Fe. Unwisely, White chose to forge ahead with his family and small group.

In October Jicarilla Apaches attacked White's party on the Santa Fe Trail. All six men, including White, were killed. The Indians kidnapped Mrs. White, her daughter, Virginia, and another woman.

On hearing of the attack, an Army rescue detail was hastily formed at Taos, New Mexico and Kit Carson, already a well known Indian tracker and fighter, selected as one of its guides.

The Apache camp was eventually located in November. Carson wanted to immediately attack the camp, possibly saving the hostages were they still alive. An Army Major, commander of the rescue party, was slightly wounded and called a halt. This delayed Carson's immediate attack of the Apaches. The Indians, on fresh mounts, easily managed to escape.

Carson and the soldiers discovered the still-warm body of Mrs. Ann White not far from the deserted camp. Judging from her body, she had been horribly abused and mistreated during captivity. Just as Carson and the rescuers approached the camp, Mrs. White had been shot through the breast with an arrow. Her small daughter, Virginia, and the other woman were never found.

Carson pointed out to his troops the exact spot where he and others had discovered Mrs. White's mutilated body.

If the usual war dance didn't interrupt the soldiers' sleep that night, Carson's graphic story about Mrs. White's captivity and heinous treatment certainly did.

15 November 1864:

Carson reassembled his column of humans, horses, mules, cattle and wagons the next morning and continued the march toward the objective area in the Texas Panhandle where the Kiowa and Comanche were believed to be wintering.

The trail led from Red River Springs to a prairie dotted with giant sand dunes. From his experience trailing the Jicarilla Apache captors of Mrs. White years earlier, Carson probably well remembered this territory.

The sands became so deep that each wagon had to be manually hauled and pushed forward. Luckily, in a few miles the sands gave way to harder terrain and the traveling became much easier.

The objective today was a camping site, chosen by Carson, called Nara Vista Springs. An alternate name selected by Lieutenant Pettis for this campsite was "Canada de Los Ruedos." Pettis chose this name due to the abundance of cottonwood trees from which replacement wagon wheels (ruedos) could be crafted and old ones repaired.

On reaching the springs, many of the soldiers not on guard or detail, stripped and jumped into the waters. At this point in the march the weather remained warm and comfortable. Despite nearing the lands of the Kiowa and their Comanche allies, Carson's Scouts continued to entertain everyone nightly with their noisy war dance.

Lieutenant Pettis wrote "...until we became accustomed to their groans and howling incident to the dance, it was impossible to sleep."

16 November 1864:

Up before daylight, the Utes and Apaches scouted ahead while the soldiers packed their gear and checked weapons prior to resuming the march.

Today's objective was a campsite called Hay Creek. After traveling some two miles from Canada de Los Ruedos, Carson announced that they had left New Mexico and were now in Texas.

From their last camp, the trail dropped away sharply, causing the men and mules more straining, sweating and swearing in order to safely ease the wagons downward through Horse Creek. The creek's far bank was soft earth, again taxing both the men and beasts.

Some seven miles from their last camp, Carson halted the column to water and rest during noontime. Later the trail passed through more sand hills and through a dry creek bed known as the Minnesota. They were about fourteen miles from the last camp. After a quarter-mile, another small creek was crossed.

A mile later Carson called a halt at Hay Creek where good water--even forage for the animals--was available. In the absence of trees the soldiers gathered dry buffalo droppings to feed their campfires. Lowering temperatures made the small fires and wool Army blankets and overcoats more valuable than ever.

17 November 1864:

Another early wake-up sounded, this time on frosty ground. The road out of Hay Creek was the best Carson had seen or remembered from his earlier travels through this part of the Panhandle. Initially the trail was graveled, then turned into a thick prairie sod.

Like all good trails this one ended in a few miles to become rolling badlands. In places the earth was uneven. In others it crumbled underfoot so that passage for humans or animals was tenuous.

A short stretch of hardened trail beckoned the Carson column into a valley, then across a small creek called the Romero and into a good campground on the opposite slope of the valley. The Romero Creek site became their encampment for the night. The lack of trees for concealment or firewood made the camp unpopular despite its plentiful spring-fed water.

During the evening Carson visited each officer and his men, talking with each group as it enjoyed hot coffee and tobacco. As usual, Carson bedded down near his Scouts after conferring briefly with Kaniache about the next day's trail.

Soldiers busily collected dried buffalo chips, just as they had at Hay Creek, to use for campfires. That night even the smoldering chips and wool blankets could not abate the cold.

The Scouts continued their dance ritual, unconcerned with either the cold or soldier complaints about their noise.

18 November 1864:

Everyone was happy to be up and moving during the chill morning after a cup of steaming, usually burned, coffee. Today the uphill trail headed northeast out of camp toward a cap rock formation, then jogged toward the east.

After crossing another creek, the column passed a small lake, where canteens were filled and animals watered.

Soon the trail split, one fork heading south, the other to the northeast. Taking the northeast fork as planned, Carson and Scouts halted the column at another good water source, the Punta de Agua Creek. They had traveled only eight miles from the last camp but the weather was worsening with snow flurries and cold winds.

19-20 November 1864:

Although this site offered little protection from the elements, Carson probably decided that a two-day rest for his force was appropriate due to fatigue, snow and cold weather.

The march since 12 November had been demanding and exhausting for everyone. Carson, known for caring for his troops, suffered without comment his own physical problems. Years before a horse had rolled over him and dragged him. His health had steadily deteriorated since that accident. After the accident, he even resolved to never ride a horse again, instead to rely on a carriage.

His resolve was short lived.

Poor rations, insufficient blankets and overcoats, inclement weather--either scorching or freezing--and the constant exertion keeping the precious supply wagons upright depleted everyone's reserves. Men and animals needed the two days rest to recoup as they neared the increasingly dangerous objective area.

During this respite, Lieutenant Pettis exercised his cannoneers and the twin howitzers. From a distance, Carson watched the lieutenant put his men through practice drill.

The sergeant on the number one gun gave the command "Load case!" at which two cannoneers hefted the appropriate round and held it, preparing for loading.

At the next command, "Load!" they simulated loading the round into the howitzer.

The sergeant crouched low, sighting down the bronze bore at an imaginary target down range. Unhappy with the sight picture, he ordered two privates to work the prolonge to shift the trail piece a few inches to the left.

Holding his hand aloft, he signaled that the howitzer was properly laid and sighted. Then he removed the rear sight. Reaching into the heavy pouch dangling from his hip, the sergeant removed a friction primer and placed it in the breech.

Stumbling to his feet, he taunted the lanyard rope.

He commanded his gun crew. "Stand clear!"

They jumped back, holding their ears as if the howitzer was going to be fired. The sergeant looked over his shoulder to Lieutenant Pettis for the signal to fire.

Pettis gave the signal and the sergeant cried, "Number one, fire!" Then he jerked the lanyard, backed off and reported to Pettis.

"Number one fired. End of mission, sir!"

Each crewmember repeated the drill until everyone could perform the "cannon hop" drill perfectly.

Pettis turned to Carson who grinned, nodding approval.

"Well done," Pettis complimented his gun crews before adding, "Now swab the bores and secure the battery."

21 November 1864:

The column, Scouts in the lead closely followed by Carson, headed southeast out of the Punta de Agua campsite. Soon they crossed another creek, the Rita Blanca, and followed a wide meadow to the southeast where cottonwoods fluttered and murmured in the cold wind.

Nearby were reminders that ancient people, perhaps shepherds or traders, had built holding pens for sheep and rudimentary stone cabins for themselves.

Four miles east of the Rita Blanca was yet another creek, Los Redos, where they elected to spend the night.

Los Redos offered an ideal winter campsite, so much so that Carson probably wished he had spent two days at Los Redos instead of Punta de Agua.

Los Redos boasted giant cottonwoods for firewood, with an east-west axis partially shielded from wintry blasts. Good water was plentiful.

Before bedding down for the night in blankets and overcoats, the troops were again serenaded by the Scouts whose war dance proved as loud and enduring as ever.

22 November 1864:

The early morning routines of loading supplies and equipment, re-saddling horses and hitching teams provided the prelude to the Scouts leading into the Los Redos Creek bed, then up the other much steeper bank. A stumpy section of plains bearing a trail to the east overlooked the creek.

Crossing the ravine on the other (east) side of the stubby section led to deeper ravines between two tributaries of the Cheyenne Creek. Still pushing east, Carson elected a new campsite just eleven miles from the previous.

Like several past campgrounds, Rica Creek offered little protection from the weather. Projected worse weather may have prompted Carson's decision to take early cover at the Rica Creek site.

23 November 1864:

This morning the column departed the campsite at Rica Creek and entered an area of low hills, leading to the northeast and the staked plains (*El Llano Estacado)* of Texas.

Enroute the troops saw circular stone designs made by early Indians. The stones were arranged as foundations for tepees. Three miles away they faced the cap rock denoting the edge of the high plains.

Atop the cap rock, the column halted to allow the wagons and drivers a brief respite to repair, refit and rest after the climb. Everyone kept weapons handy and alert to their surroundings in case hostiles might be waiting in ambush. From the cap rock, everyone could plainly see the entire route they had taken during the previous days.

Two miles more and a small natural lake appeared on the right where a rest stop was ordered. Later, back in the saddle, the troops inched their way down a rough tangled, slope overgrown with cactus and yucca. Carson chose a new campsite near the Blue (also called the

Azul) Creek. The site's location provided a good defensive position yet was partially sheltered from the cold wind.

Carson detailed several sentinels to the high bluffs to the east where observation was excellent. Those troops not on guard duty, had coffee, hardtack, and smokes prior to rolling in their blankets and overcoats.

Due to the proximity of Blue Creek to the objective area, this would be the last night for the Scouts' war dance. Although no one knew it, this would also be the last full night of rest for everyone.

24 November 1864:

Today was the second celebration of the new national holiday called Thanksgiving. The holiday passed unnoticed as Carson's men prepared to advance farther into hostile territory.

Lieutenanr Pettis inaccurately remembered in his narratives that the Carson command had "marched through the State of Texas and arrived at the western part of the Indian Territory."

That evening the Scouts sitting in camp suddenly stood and pointed to the east where two riders could barely be seen, approaching on horseback.

It was two returning Scouts who rode through the camp without comment until they reached Carson. They reported finding a large Indian presence with horses and cattle in the area several miles ahead they had observed that morning.

Carson immediately organized for combat. His lead element would be himself, the Scouts, the two howitzers and crews plus the mounted troops.

He would lead a night march toward the Canadian River and the area reported by the two Scouts.

Staying behind at Mule Creek would be Lieutenant Colonel Abreu's infantrymen, some of the dismounted cavalrymen and their invaluable wagon trains. Abreu would lead the trains forward to a good defensive position of his choosing after following Carson's trail in the morning.

MOVEMENT TO CONTACT

24 November 1864:

Carson and Scouts led the way in the frosty but clear moonlit night to the southeast. Finding an arroyo leading to the river, they silently picked their way down the rough slopes as silently as possible.

Previously Carson had given the terse order "no smoking, no talking."

After slowly meandering toward the Canadian River for approximately ten miles, Carson halted the column and sent his Scouts forward for more information concerning the enemy.

"Before twelve," Pettis wrote, "we had descended again into the valley of the Canadian...and had found in the dark, the deep-worn, fresh trail of the hostile Indians.

"At this time, we believed that we were in the immediate vicinity of the enemy, and as nothing of their position was known to us, it was deemed prudent to remain where we were, and move on again just before daylight.

"No talking was allowed, the few orders that were necessary were given in a whisper. Lighting of pipes and smoking were prohibited. Each officer and soldier, upon halting, only dismounted, and remained holding his horse by the bridle rein until morning; and to add to our discomforts a heavy frost fell during the night."

Remembering their previous night's rest, the troops stood beside their horses, reins in hand, instructed to keep their animals quiet while awaiting the new day, new orders and new dangers.

As the night was ebbing, the Scouts returned from the river with new intelligence for Carson.

With relief, the troops saw the hand signal to mount their ponies after standing beside them throughout the cold and silent night.

As soon as they moved forward, they found themselves on the bank of the river. All around them tall grasses grew in abundance, some as high as a mounted rider's head. Carson and Pettis, riding alongside each other, could barely make out the other.

Carson confided to Pettis of a recent vision. "I had a dream the night before, of being engaged with a large number of Indians; your cannons were firing." Chuckling, Carson wiped his eyes with a gritty kerchief.

In two miles the high bluffs alongside the riverbank gave way to rolling, hills and Carson nudged his horse out of the tall grasses and onto more solid footing.

RECONNAISANCE BY FIRE

25 November 1864:

At that moment came a clear, chilling challenge from across the river. Indian warriors were repeating the Spanish phrase, "Vene aca! Vene aca! (Come here!)"

Carson immediately ordered Major William McCleave to lead Company B (California Cavalry) and Captain Charles Deus' Company M, (First Cavalry, New Mexico Volunteers) across the river to engage the taunting warriors.

Carson probably realized that the warriors were attempting to divert his attention from their nearby villages on Carson's side of the river.

Rapid small arms fire announced a fight had begun on the other (south) side of the river. The Ute and Apache Scouts shed their buffalo robes and rushed into the river. Without robes, their war paint and feathers plainly announced their appetite for battle.

Carson led his remaining element further up the north side of the river until he could see a large Indian village some five miles in the distance. Turning to Captain Emil Fritz (First Cavalry, California Volunteers), he ordered him to reinforce Major McCleave, now pursuing warriors on the north side of the river.

Manhandling the two mountain howitzers in the north river bank's high grass and weeds proved exhausting for Pettis' cannoneers since the caisson carriages on which the howitzers were mounted tipped over easily. The carriages upon which the howitzers were mounted were too small for the cannoneers to ride, so they had to double time beside their howitzers. The cavalry quickly outdistanced the heavily breathing artillerymen.

The Mountain Howitzer M1841

Up ahead, the Scouts busily claimed booty from a herd of Kiowa horses encountered. Each Scout would replace his tired mount with a fresh pony chosen from the herd and mark others as belonging to him on their return from battle. Such compensation had been the Scouts' bargain with Carson back at the Cimarron ranch.

Still pushing up the north side of the river, Carson spotted the Kiowa camp now about two miles away. It was a sprawling winter camp of approximately 150-200 lodges or tepees, glistening white in the rays of the rising sun.

Lieutenant Pettis, unfamiliar with Plains Indians, mistook their buffalo hide tepees for U.S. Army Sibley tents of similar design. Later he would learn much more about the oficer-designer of those Army tents.

Pettis' mistake about the tepees later caused Carson a good laugh. The U.S. Army Sibley tent was named for *Union* Colonel--later *Confederate* Brigadier General--Sibley whose rebel force Carson fought at the battle of Valverde, New Mexico.

Sibley had led an invading force of Texans with an audacious plan to add New Mexico, maybe even California, to the Confederacy.

Sibley's grandiose plan failed and his force eventually limped back to Texas after heavy losses.

Chuckling, Carson punched Pettis' shoulder. "I've a story to tell you someday about *thet* feller."

The Kiowas' surprise at finding McCleave and Carson outside their camp was short lived. Warriors bolted to their horses to fight McCleave, while Kiowa women, children and the elderly fled for shelter in the sand hills northwest of their overrun, being-deserted village.

Kiowa Chief Dohasan, whose camp was invaded, gathered his warriors and sent messengers to warn the Comanche villages several miles down river to the northeast. Chased by McCleave's troopers, the Chief led his warriors toward the ruins of an old trading post, known as Adobe Walls.

KIOWA PRINCIPAL CHIEF DOHASAN OR SERRITO WHO
DIRECTED THE KIOWA ATTACKS AGAINST CARSON'S
OUTNUMBERED COMMAND. (Courtesy: Wikipedia Commons)

Indian trader William Bent had constructed a trading post/fort/ saloon of thick adobe bricks between the Canadian River and a small creek in 1845. The thick-walled structure served alternately as a trading post and fort. Originally its dimensions were only eighty feet by eighty feet. The walls were a good nine feet tall. Bent had added to his original 80X80 plan several times.

Becoming exasperated with the volatile, often dangerous Indian trade, Bent blew up the interior of the fort in 1865 and moved to Colorado where he had other business interests.

Carson studied the ruins with interest. He had been there twenty years before when he hunted buffalo for the Bents in the Texas high plains.

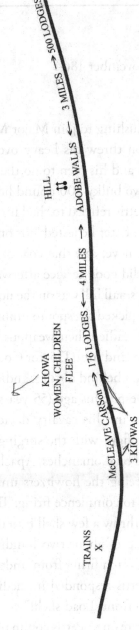

FIRST BATTLE OF ADOBE WALLS, 25 NOV 1564

CANADIAN RIVER
(NOT TO SCALE)

500 LODGES
3 MILES
ADOBE WALLS
HILL
4 MILES
176 LODGES
KIOWA WOMEN, CHILDREN FLEE
McCLEAVE CARSon
3 KIOWAS
TRAINS X

1000 hrs: Pettis estimate 200 attacking warriors
1500 hrs: Pettis estimates 3000 attacking warriors
1530 hrs: Carson orders withdrawal

ESTABLISHING A FIRE BASE

25 November 1864

Rushing to join Major McCleave in the fight before Adobe Walls, Carson threw his heavy overcoat onto a bush and urged Lieutenant Pettis and his men to do the same as they doggedly attempted to rush the two bulky 500 pound howitzers forward.

Pettis refused to shed his coat and told his men not to dump theirs, either. Later he jested "for once my judgment was better than Carson's for he never saw that coat of his again, while my own and those of my men did good service afterwards."

A small hill was on the northeast a short distance from Adobe Walls. Pettis picked the spot to unlimber the two mountain howitzers. His gun crews readied their weapons for action.

Behind him, Doctor Courtright was setting up his aid station/field hospital behind a still-standing corner of the adobe walls.

Despite his age (55 years) and old injuries, Carson led Lieutenant Heath and his cavalry detachment forward to join Major McCleave in the fight with the surging, mounted Kiowa warriors already being joined by Comanches, Apaches and Arapahoes.

Seeing the howitzers unhitched and positioned, Carson yelled at Pettis to commence firing. The time was about 1000 hours.

"Throw a few shell into that crowd over *thar*!" He gestured toward a group of about two hundred warriors racing back and forth before them, often firing from under the necks of their horses.

Pettis responded immediately as did his two gun crews. "Battery, action front! Load shell!"

"Fire one," Pettis commanded in moments. "Fire two!" The resultant booms momentarily silenced the din from the hostiles who had never seen nor heard cannon fire.

They stood up in their rawhide stirrups to stare at the strange howitzers. Initially mesmerized by the devastating noise and effect of the twelve-pound shells, they quickly realized their danger, swirled about and rode back toward their village.

In plain sight from his position, Pettis could see a much larger Comanche village of approximately 500 lodges only a mile behind the retreating warriors.

Years later Pettis wrote, in the only eye-witness account of the first battle of Adobe Walls "when the fourth shot (from the howitzers) was fired there was not a single enemy within the extreme range of the howitzers."

Later the warriors described the howitzers as the guns that "spoke twice." The first explosion was the shell exiting the bore of the howitzer. The second boom was the detonation of the explosive shell on its target. The effect on horses and warriors was deadly.

Seeing the warriors scatter and ride away, Carson assumed that the battle was over. He dismounted his cavalry near the Adobe Walls ruin as skirmishers. Mounts were unsaddled or unhitched and watered in the nearby stream, whose banks abounded with grass.

Doctor Courtright's "hospital" behind a corner of the ruins began treating the wounded stumbling toward it. Meanwhile ammunition was being re-supplied, canteens filled and haversacks explored by the hungry soldiers for hardtack or raw bacon.

The walls of the old trading post also partially sheltered horses and mules being returned from watering at the nearby creek.

The battle was far from over. Through his field glasses atop a small rise Carson saw large bands of warriors already returning to the battle. He quickly ordered Pettis to hitch-up his cannon and again emplace the two howitzers on the hill.

Alerting the skirmishers circling the ruins, Carson readied his command for more attacks.

The howitzers began firing again as the throng of Kiowas and Comanches approached within range.

The first cannon fired and the second followed in a few seconds. Rammers sponged-out cannon bores to prevent cook-off of rounds.

Loaders stumbled forward, carrying fresh ammunition while sergeants re-checked the lay of the cannon even as loaders slammed rounds into the breech.

The cannon were primed and crews ordered back. Recoil from the firing knocked each howitzer momentarily into the air and backward. The quick dance of the crewmen to ready the howitzer for another round was repeated over and over.

This time the howitzer fire was not as effective as previously. The Comanche and Kiowa chiefs quickly had warned their warriors to spread out more than usual. This increased the distance between charging warriors, creating less of an area target for Pettis' gunners. Fewer casualties fell from each round fired.

Pettis estimate of the warriors facing them by mid-afternoon was 1400 combined Kiowas and Comanches. Also among the surging warriors were some Arapaho and Apache.

A bugle suddenly rang out from behind the horde of charging warriors. Bewildered, Carson's soldiers looked at each other. Their own bugler, there alongside them, certainly had not played.

An Indian was proficiently playing an Army bugle but reversing the calls of Carson's bugler. If Carson's bugler blew "Charge!" the Indian bugler would play the call for "Retreat!"

Carson and his troops shook their heads at the counterfeit bugle calls, then began grinning. They soon realized from where the calls were coming. Hilarity on the battlefield--rather than confusion--resulted.

Carson initially claimed that a white man was playing the deceptive bugle calls. His officers opined that the fake bugle calls were made by a Kiowa named Satanta, one of Chief Dohasan's sub-chiefs.

Despite the howitzers' booming and the continual small arms fire from Carson's dismounted troops, the Comanches and Kiowas kept charging on horseback.

In the tall grass, Carson hunkered down the firing line, urging his troops to concentrate their fire on the closer, charging lines, not on the masses of warriors behind them. His calm presence reassured his men, improving both their morale and marksmanship.

WITHDRAWAL

---

25 November 1864:

By that afternoon Carson was keenly aware of the mounting shortages of ammunition, particularly for the howitzers, and water. The bores of the two howitzers were smoking and many of his soldiers had dry canteens despite the proximity of water temporarily unreachable because of the intensity of combat.

Although he had no casualty count as yet, Carson was concerned about the number of his killed and wounded.

He and Kaniache exchanged words and nods about the festering situation before them. The Ute chief made clear with raised fingers what he considered to be the strength of the enemy relative to Carson's. Ten fingers, he held up.

Then only one.

Pettis remembered and described the scene well. "Quite a number of the enemy acted as skirmishers, being dismounted and hid in the tall grass in our front, and made it hot for most of us by their excellent marksmanship, while quite the larger part of them, mounted and covered with their war dresses, charged continually across our front, from right to left and vice versa, about two hundred yards from our line of skirmishers, yelling like demons, and firing from under the necks of their horses at intervals."

On or about 1500 hours that afternoon, Pettis estimated the enemy strength had increased to 3,000 warriors being led by Comanche Chief Ten Bears as well as the Kiowa principal Chief, Dohasan.

Chief Ten Bears later made the following accusation about the Adobe Walls battle at a meeting with the Peace Commission from Washington in 1867:

"My people have never first drawn a bow or fired a gun against the whites. There has been trouble between us…My young men have danced the war dance. But it was not begun by us.

"It was you who sent out the first soldier. The blue-dressed soldiers and the Utes came out from the night…and for campfires they lit our tepees."

Carson's advance force consisting of 12 officers, 263 troopers and 75 Indian Scouts was vastly outnumbered by the combined Kiowa, Comanche, Apache and Arapaho.

"Most of our officers," Pettis recorded "were anxious to press on and capture the villages immediately in our front, and Carson was at one time about to give orders to that effect, when our Indians prevailed upon him to return and completely destroy the village that we had already captured…"

Minutes later at about 1530 hours, Carson made a fateful decision. He ordered his men to regroup and withdraw back to the west toward the Kiowa camp.

Officers split their men into groups of four. One man took the reins and led all four horses while the other three troopers acted as dismounted riflemen on either side of their mounts.

To further protect the flanks of his formation, Carson ordered Captain Fritz's Company B, First Cavalry, California Volunteers, to screen the right.

On the formation's left flank, he placed Captain Witham and Company M, First California Cavalry. A portion of Captain Charles Deus' company of the First Cavalry, New Mexico Volunteers, reinforced Company M.

Protecting the rear of the formation was the mission of Captain Joseph Berney and Company D, First New Mexico Cavalry. Also at the rear was the remainder of Captain Deus' company.

At the back of the column were the caissons/carriages bearing the two mountain howitzers of Lieutenant Pettis' battery.

Doctor Courtright and the wounded were sandwiched into the center of the formation. At that point two dead troopers and ten wounded were identified. Among the Scouts, one had been killed and five wounded.

Carson headed his force back toward the Kiowa village where they would complete the destruction of the lodges and all contents.

Frenzied that their homes, food for the winter, clothing and all belongings would be destroyed--leaving them and their families bereft during the coldest part of the year--the warriors charged Carson's formation with renewed vigor.

"The Indians charged us so repeatedly and with such desperation that for some time I had serious doubts for the safety of my rear," Carson later confided.

The troopers reacted in kind, placing constant aimed fire on the charging warriors. Each charge was repelled with severe casualties.

Seeing the mounted charges were less and less effective, the chiefs ordered their warriors to set grass fires along the river beside Carson's column. The warriors used the smoke as a screen to tear at Carson's flanks without being seen. One of Carson's men was lanced and several others were wounded during the smoke and gunfire exchanges. The prevailing east winds and the dense smoke made it harder for Carson's troopers to pick out targets among the attacking Indians.

Despite the smokescreen, one warrior's attempt to kill a soldier failed. A sudden change in the wind exposed this warrior's position. Facing a young New Mexico volunteer, the warrior fired but missed. The young soldier shot the Indian from his horse, then scalped the fallen warrior. Comrades of the young soldier prevented other warriors from snatching and riding away with the dead or wounded warrior as was their custom.

This was the only scalp--an enemy one--taken during the First Battle of Adobe Walls.

Carson motioned his troops to veer to the right to higher terrain, slightly out of the billowing black smoke.

To provide clearance ahead, he had several soldiers fire the grass ahead of their column.

Lieutenant Pettis employed his howitzers on a higher elevation and began shelling the warriors attacking the rear of the column.

Another group of warriors was already in the village, ahead of Carson and the column. The Kiowas were frantically saving what provisions they could.

Once near the Kiowa village near sundown, soldiers assumed firing positions on the sandy knoll overlooking the camp. The warriors attempting to salvage what goods they could from their village became easy targets for the bluecoats.

Pettis' howitzers next were manhandled to the top of a small hill, selected by Carson, and again began shelling the scrambling warriors. After a round was fired, the howitzer would recoil down the back of the hill, to be replaced by the other cannon pushed back up the hill and fired.

While the skirmishers fired into the thronging warriors, other troops began burning all the Kiowa camp's stores, food, gunpowder, trade goods, even the tepees and ridge poles.

In one lodge an elderly Apache chief named Iron Shirt refused all demands to leave his tepee. The frustrated troopers shot him in front of his lodge.

They discovered a cache of tanned buffalo robes in the village and every soldier grabbed at least one. Carson, who forgot to retrieve his issue overcoat left on a mesquite bush hours before, took one of the warm robes for himself.

Among the strangest items destroyed in the village were a buggy and wagon presented to Chief Dohasan as a token of friendship by an Army unit in Kansas.

Two old Ute squaws were among Carson's Scouts. During the sacking of the Kiowa camp, the squaws discovered two blind and two crippled Kiowas, deserted during the hasty exodus from the village. The squaws gleefully killed the four with axes unknown to Carson until later.

The cannon spoke again, shells falling among the warriors escaping from the south end of the village and running toward the river. The howitzer rounds whistled in the darkening skies. Finally the warriors began to relent and fall back.

Destruction of the Kiowa village containing 176 counted lodges completed, Carson and the Scouts regrouped to lead the formation westward in search of Lieutenant Colonel Abreu's defensive position. Abreu, seventy-five infantry and some cavalry, had been left behind to protect the precious wagon train.

By then it was dark. Carson's troops were dog-tired having fought for thirty hours without respite and missing two nights sleep without the usual war dance.

Little had been eaten since the battle commenced on the 24th leaving the men ravenously hungry and fatigued but still alert for Indian ambush or attack.

To slightly improve their comfort, the wounded were placed on howitzer caissons and ammunition carts. A roll call was taken and the resultant casualty count was two bluecoats killed in action, (KIA), and ten wounded in action, (WIA).

In two more miles the smoke-blackened soldiers reached the location where Carson and Pettis had initially spotted the Kiowa village in the distance.

"The march now became the most unpleasant part of the day's operation," Pettis recalled. "The wounded were suffering severely; the men and horses were completely worn out; the enemy might attack us at any moment, unseen; and the uncertainty of the whereabouts and condition of our wagon train, for you will remember that we were now nearly two hundred and fifty miles from the nearest habitation, or hopes of supply, with the whole Comanche and Kiowa nations at our heels— all combined to make it anything but a pleasant situation to be in."

Trudging onward, Carson encouraged his officers and men to keep moving toward a well-deserved rest somewhere ahead in Abreu's trains area.

In three more hours, a glimmer of lights on their right front pinpointed what Carson hoped was Abreu's position. He paused. Could it instead be a hostile Indian camp?

Everyone was grateful to hear a soldier's challenge: "HALT, who goes there?" as they neared the lights.

REST AND RECUPERATION

26 November 1864:

   In the confusion of the withdrawal Carson completely forgot about the warm overcoat he'd tossed onto a bush as the fight first began. Wearing the buffalo robe he'd snatched at the Kiowa village, he rode all through the night.

   He'd been in the saddle almost four days. Carson's fatigue was more evident on his poor horse. When he thankfully dismounted later in the trains area, he removed the saddle from his mount. The saddle blanket brought off with it a large section of the weary horse's skin.

   Once inside Abreu's defense perimeter, horses were unsaddled or unhitched, fires fanned to life for hot coffee, canteens topped-off and blankets shaken out. The majority of the returnees were more interested in sleep than food. The campsite was suddenly quiet as exhausted men fell to the ground and slept.

   Meanwhile, the officers assembled around Carson. Several sharply questioned their commander.

   Why had he ordered a withdrawal instead of continuing along the river, attacking and destroying the larger Comanche camps just a few miles distant from the adobe ruins?

   Carson cut short the discussion. "I'll answer you *jest* as soon as I think we're safe from reprisal attacks."

   The officers glanced at each other uneasily. Carson seldom used such a curt tone.

   "For the moment," he changed the subject, "I'd like to hear your assessments of Kiowa and Comanche strengths and casualties.

   "As you probably have heard, we had two KIA. Privates Sullivan and O'Donnell, both of "M" Company, were killed. Twenty-one soldiers--including ten wounded--are being treated by our surgeon *ratt* now.

"In addition to our soldiers, we lost one Scout killed and five wounded."

"Plus a large number of horses injured, wounded," Major McCleave added. "Or killed."

Carson nodded, then turned to look at the closest officer. "Lieutenant Heath, what's your estimate of the hostiles' strength and casualties?"

Heath swallowed. "I guess that we faced 1300 to 1400 warriors in the early afternoon, sir. I thought by the middle of the afternoon their strength had grown to 3,000. Lieutenant Pettis also thought he saw 3,000. As to casualties, I heard tell that at least 100 hostiles were killed or wounded."

"Who said that?"

"I heard it from one of our Scouts. What's your estimate, Sir?"

"Well, I reckon the chiefs had maybe 1000 warriors among both tribes. More than sixty were killed and wounded."

Carson coughed. "I'm guessing, just like you."

He swallowed a hot sip of coffee from a tin cup offered him. "We may have been outnumbered close to ten to one, gents," he frowned, either at the hot coffee or his estimates.

"Maybe the hostiles had sixty casualties. *Jest* a guess."

Major McCleave spoke up. "I'd say Lieutenant Heath's estimate is just about right, Colonel. I'd never seen *so many Indians!*

"And I hope to never see that many again!"

Those officers not nodding in agreement chuckled at McCleave's expression.

Carson stood, signaling the end of the session. "Now…Check your men, weapons and don't forget our horses.

"Then *you* get some rest. I'm anxious to be out of here before first light."

He turned to Abreu. "My congratulations, Colonel, on selecting such a good defensive position here. I thank you and your men for providing double security while the rest of us sleep tonight."

Carson paused, turning to warn the group before dismissal. "Ain't no way the hostiles don't know exactly where we're at *ratt* now! I expect each of you to be as alert as a mountain cat! And keep your men the same way!"

As the officers dispersed, returning to their units, Carson limped over toward Doctor Courtright where he and his helpers tended to the wounded.

"How're they doin', Doc?"

Courtright looked up from drying his hands. "I hope they'll all make it through the night, Colonel," he whispered.

"I'm sure we'll have several more men needing attention once they're awake in the morning."

An attendant offered cups of coffee to Carson and Courtright squatting on the ground.

"Much obliged," Carson thanked the man.

Courtright nodded thanks before rubbing his forehead, his usual prelude to a story.

"You hear about our snake bit soldier?" He grinned at the recollection.

"Snake bit?" Carson frowned. "No, I ain't heard."

Shaking his head, Courtright began.

"Yesterday when we were clustered around Adobe Walls warding off those wild charges, one of our young New Mexico volunteers was bitten on the little finger by a rattlesnake. He came to our makeshift hospital behind the wall. Hand was already swelling.

"Well, I examined him. Did what I could to draw off the poison, cauterized it and bandaged the hand. I gave him a good shot of whisky, too. Then I made him lay down with the wounded for a spell.

"In an hour or so, he seemed fine. So I sent him back to his unit. I got to see him briefly just as we pulled into here. He's still fit and mighty anxious to get home.

"I'll point him out to you tomorrow if you like."

"I'd be pleased to shake his hand, Doc," Carson finished his coffee and stood.

"I mean the hand not snake bit, of course."

27 November 1864:

Carson later wrote "I now decided that owing to the broken-down condition of my cavalry horses and transportation and the Indians having fled in all directions with their stock that it was impossible for me to chastise them further at present. Therefore, on the morning of the 27th...I broke camp and commenced my return trip."

The bugler--the real Army bugler--sounded reveille earlier than usual that morning per Carson's instructions. Everyone was up and alert, aware that the Kiowa/Comanche favorite time to attack was before dawn.

The Scouts rode into camp in the early morning gloom. Surprisingly, they reported seeing no signs of activity.

Relieved, Carson allowed the men to prepare as much food as they had left for their first full meal in several days.

As the sun crested the horizon, a group of Kiowa and Comanche warriors on horseback ominously appeared on a ridge two miles away. Kaniache and the Scouts quickly jumped on their ponies and rode east to meet the challengers.

With yells and motions, the two groups insulted each other from a distance for several minutes. Then they exchanged a few random shots without effect.

Suddenly the Comanches and Kiowas wheeled their horses about and headed back east.

Hoping the threat was over, Carson instructed troopers to check and maintain their weapons and equipment. Special attention was given the exhausted horses and mules, ridden hard since 12 November.

A group of the Ute and Apache Scouts stood around one young soldier, bartering for something the soldier held in his hand.

Carson watched them curiously. "What's that?"

"Colonel, that's the man who killed and scalped a warrior yesterday." Captain Berney answered proudly. "One of my men, Sir."

Doctor Courtright overhead the exchange. "Well, gads! That's the same man who got snake bit! The one I told you about, Colonel," he exclaimed.

"Ought to think about promoting that man to corporal, Captain," Carson turned to Berney. "Not only did he survive a rattlesnake bite, he also took the only scalp!"

Holding high the scalp just purchased from the soldier, the Scouts whooped and waved their weapons. On subsequent evenings the war dance--celebrating the enemy scalp the Scouts had just purchased-- would be extra loud and exuberant.

But not that night. Even the Scouts were so tired they postponed their usual war dance.

Early the next morning the bugler played reveille, followed an hour later by "boots and saddles." Carson dispatched Scouts ahead as well as to the rear to watch for hostiles.

He ordered a slow march westward to benefit his suffering wounded men, horses and mules.

The back trail was easy to follow, furrows made by the wagons and artillery as well as bent grasses pointing the way home. Good water waited at each of the campsites Carson planned to occupy on the way west.

REMEMBERING VALVERDE

30 November 1864:

The next evening Carson called his officers together to respond to their criticisms of his order to withdraw. Instead of withdrawing, several officers had wanted to continue the advance along the Canadian River to attack and destroy the larger Comanche encampments just a few miles down river from the razed Kiowa village.

Lighting his pipe he began speaking between draws. "I appreciate your questioning my order to withdraw the other day rather than attack. In other armies, nobody questions the battlefield decisions of their dukes or princes or whatever. Thank goodness, we do.

"I begin my talk to you tonight--and its plumb likely to be a long one--with a phrase I learned long ago when President Polk told me he was nominating me for a lieutenant's commission.

"He told me he had implicit faith in my ability and devotion to the nation. He also raised an important point that's worth remembering by every one of you. If you expect to excel in the Army, that is. That's why I'm keeping you from your men and duties right now.

"Here it is. Orders are orders! Obey them! Simple, ain't it?

"You may not always understand those orders but your duty is to obey them to the best of your ability before belly-bloating about them.

"What I'm about to tell you is an attempt to teach you to rely on your commander's decisions. Usually he's more advanced in years of service, in age and experience, and of course, in rank, than you.

"So here's my story about how I once objected to the orders of my commander at Valverde just like some of you did at Adobe Walls.

"But I obeyed them. They were orders.

"Later I found out the reasons for his order--which I thought porely at the time--were as good as gold.

"Cookie," Carson called to a nearby cook. "Better boil up a big pot of coffee for this bunch. We're going to be here talkin' for some time."

Carson cleared his throat and sat down in the midst of the group. "I hope you're excusing my not standing," he said, looking about him.

"I'm like the old peddler at the country store trying to sell a lady's corset. I can't get into it without sittin'."

Few smiles followed the attempt at humor. His audience held their breath awaiting the serious words--maybe reprimands—sure to follow.

Carson cleared his throat again. "I ain't a graduate of the Military Academy at West Point. Neither, I recollect, are any of you," he surveyed their faces again.

"A little history, gentlemen. Secession was the South's attempt to break apart our Union. Secession divided our government. Why, our nation's Secretary of War from '53-'57 was Jeff Davis, a graduate of the Military Academy class of '28. He performed mighty good Army service during our war with Mexico. Then Davis resigned his government job and joined the rebs. He even became their president.

"Like our government, our Army fell apart over secession. For example, two Military Academy friends were Canby, class of '39, and Sibley, class of '38."

Carson nodded at Lieutenant Pettis. "You remember those Kiowa tepees you mistook for Sibley army tents? Same Sibley.

"The two of 'em, both West Point graduates, Canby and Sibley. Why even their families were good friends.

"The two men were not just chums. Canby was best man at Sibley's wedding! Their wives were cousins! That's how close they were. Until secession.

"Then they chose different sides and became enemies: *Union* Colonel Canby and *Confederate* Brigadier General Sibley. They fought each other in the New Mexico desert north of Mesilla, at a places called Fort Craig and Valverde on the Rio Grande River."

Carson noticed one of his officers hiding a yawn. "Hold on, Captain Witham," he chided. "I'm comin' around the turn and runnin' fast.

"Now, Colonel Canby commanded the Union garrison at Fort Craig including me and my First New Mexico Infantry Regiment of Volunteers. Had ten companies in my regiment.

"General Sibley invaded New Mexico with four cavalry regiments totaling about three thousand rebs from Texas. Fort Craig was the first of Sibley's main objectives.

"Sibley's grandiose plan, which he somehow convinced Confederate President Jeff Davis—-West Point class of '28, remember--to approve, was to invade New Mexico. Sibley expected his Texas troops to be *welcomed* in New Mexico as liberators!

"Knowledge of your enemy is as necessary as a bath at Christmas time. Sibley, being a Louisianian, didn't fully understand that most New Mexicans feel about Texans like ponies feel about purple horse flies. They can't stand them!

"Sibley expected his brigade to be so welcome in New Mexico that it could live off the local crops and friendly, hospitable civilians. His regular supplies, food, ammunition and such, had to come all the way from El Paso. His home base, San Antonio, was even farther, a whole thousand miles away.

"Fort Craig is a stoutly-built and fortified post. Canby was well situated there, expecting--even preparing—-to be attacked by Sibley and his so-called 'Army of New Mexico.'

"Canby fortified and revetted around Fort Craig. Inside he commanded almost 4,000 men, so he was well off compared to Sibley. Also in Canby's favor were stockpiles of rations, medical supplies, ammunition and plenty of water.

"Supply trains from Santa Fe kept Canby provisioned on a regular basis. In fact a train of seventy wagons delivered him supplies on 14 February 1862. The battle began two days later, on the 16th.

"Fort Craig would be a tough nut to crack. All Canby had to do was stay inside those thick fort walls ringed by his sharpshooters. He even had plenty of artillery: both 12 and 24-pounders to reach out and bloody attacking formations.

"Sibley's troops, on the other hand, were not as well armed nor provisioned. Water was in constant short supply both for his two-legged and four-legged critters.

"As you gents well know," Carson studied their faces, "how necessary fresh, abundant water is for mounted operations.

"That's why on our way to Adobe Walls, we overnighted at good springs and *cricks*. Sibley wasn't as fortunate out there in the New Mexican desert. His supply planning wasn't near as good as Canby's.

"Knowin' Fort Craig from previous assignments in New Mexico, Sibley doubted he could overwhelm the place by frontal assault.

"So he knew he had to dupe Canby into coming *outside* his fortified post."

Carson waved at the cook staggering under the weight of a big caldron of hot coffee. "C'mon over, Cookie! And thank you!

"Help yourselves, gentlemen, to hot coffee before I get into comparin' Valverde with Adobe Walls.

"So…here we go with a near battle outside Fort Craig.

"On the morning of the 16th one of Sibley's regiments, the 5th, commanded by a colonel named Tom Green deployed in textbook, West Point style outside Fort Craig. The Fort looked quiet, even appeared deserted.

"Suddenly Fort Craig came alive! The U.S. colors were raised, bugles sounded and infantry ran out to occupy the new earthworks in front of their fort.

"Several Union cavalry units rushed outside the gates and feinted at Green's left flank. After firing several volleys, Canby's cavalrymen wheeled about and rode back inside the fort.

"Disgusted by the lack of action, Green ordered his dusty, thirsty and exasperated Texas troops to return to their inhospitable, dry sand camp.

"But Green wasn't through. He suggested a plan to General Sibley, who already had traded his saddle for the comforts of a hospital wagon. Sibley said the reason was 'illness.' The real reason was his heavy drinkin'.

"Green's plan, which Sibley approved, was to cross the frozen Rio Grande River, well out of sight of Fort Craig, to the eastern side. Then

Green would lead Sibley's force on a loop-around trail leading to an important river crossing called Valverde, six miles north of the fort.

"That Valverde crossing was important since it straddled Canby's main supply route.

"If his supplies were choked off at Valverde, Canby might be forced to come out of his fortress and fight Sibley in the open.

"The Texans' first camp on the loop-around trail was atop a sand dune directly east of Fort Craig. While the Texans watched twenty-five Union companies emerged from their fort, crossed the river and deployed for the attack.

"Green countered the Union threat by placing his companies and artillery in positions along a ridgeline, hoping Canby really intended to fight.

"Adding to the occasion, Confederate battle flags were unfurled, the band of the 5th Texas played "Dixie" and Texas artillery began firing at the Union formations.

"Canby's troops responded by returning small arms and artillery fire before re-crossing the cold river and returning to their comfortable, if crowded, fort.

"Suspecting Sibley's demonstration was to disguise his real plan to surprise-attack Fort Craig, Colonel Canby wisely dispatched me and my New Mexico volunteers to the eastside of the river, to some high bluffs opposite Fort Craig where we could observe and report Sibley's actions."

Carson rose to refill his tin cup from the giant coffeepot. Before resuming his place, he studied the reactions of his officers. Some looked thoughtful; others, tense. Several appeared bored.

Tin cup in one hand and a burned stick in the other, Carson began outlining the opposing positions at Valverde. He sketched the positions on the back of the hanging, whitened buffalo robe he had grabbed at the Kiowa village.

"So I led several companies across the river at this point," he rubbed the charcoal stick against the whitened side of the robe.

"We secured a mighty fine observation point 'bout here on the high bluffs 'cross the river from the Fort," he pointed, "without any trouble.

"From there we could see everything the Texans were doing which *wuz* mostly quarreling and frettin' about the lack of water for them and their mounts.

"From what I could tell, they intended moving northward toward the Valverde crossing, not directly at Fort Craig. One of my captains wrote down our observations and we sent them by messenger down to Colonel Canby. We also tried sending semaphore signals to him from our bluffs.

"Sibley's troops thought they were hidden from observation from Fort Craig by the huge basalt hill called Mesa de la Contadera. But we could see 'em fine from our observation post.

"The rebs started inching toward Valverde *jest* like I figured. Their second dry camp was just to the east of that crossing.

"I talked earlier about the importance of knowing your enemy, remember? Knowing the water crisis among Sibley's troops, horses and mules was as useful as holdin' a sharp knife during a brawl.

"Canby had a company called the Graydon Independent Spy Company. Captain James "Paddy" Graydon came up with an imaginative plan to stampede Sibley's water-starved stock to the river where they could be corralled by our troops.

"Without horses and mules, Sibley would be in a fit. His mounted cavalry regiments would suddenly become infantrymen, just like most of Canby's force.

"Graydon picked two scrawny mules, tied wooden crates containing a bunch of twenty-four pound artillery shells to their backs, intending to run the mules, shell fuses burning, into the rebels' herd.

"On hearing the exploding cannon balls, those thirst-starved mules of the Texas 4th Mounted Regiment would panic and stampede westward toward the smell of water, the Rio Grande.

"For the cost of two mules and a dozen artillery shells Canby might capture many of Sibley's water-starved mounts. Canby's men would simply police up the mules and horses along the river after they drank their fill, then corral them at Fort Craig, their new home."

Suddenly Carson straightened, looking around him. "Guess what happened?"

Initially, his audience looked aghast, not expecting to be questioned by their commander. The silence lasted a full minute until Captain Deus raised a hand.

Deus grinned. "I bet the two mules with the explosives smelled the water and ran for the river behind them *instead* of toward the rebs.

"And got blown to kingdom come before they got their noses wet in the Rio Grande," he scoffed.

"Good guess, Captain," Carson grinned as the others cackled.

"Captain Graydon's detail succeeded in quietly getting those two mules real close to the Texas camp. One man lit the fuses hanging from the two crates. Immediately, another man slapped the mules hard on the butt. Off the two went running toward the Texas herd just as planned.

"Suddenly the two mules stopped. Something about the Texas mules must have seemed odd, maybe unfamiliar, so the two turned around and started chasing the panicking Graydon and his men!

"Riding for their lives, Graydon's men set new records trying to stay ahead of those two mules and their explosive-filled barrels!

"Lucky for them, the artillery shells exploded killing the two mules before catching up with Graydon's terrified detail.

"Even so, Paddy's crazy plan was successful! The explosion really excited some 150 wild-eyed, thirsty but otherwise healthy Texas mules. They stampeded toward the smell of water in the Rio Grande.

"The loss of those mules stranded some thirty of Sibley's wagons loaded with rations, equipment and ammunition. The thirty wagonloads had to be redistributed and the thirty wagons and their remaining contents burned. Our patrols rounded up the no-longer thirsty Texas mules along the riverbank and herded them into to Fort Craig.

"Now to the battle about to start at the Valverde crossing. Based on our reports, Canby sent a mixed infantry, cavalry and artillery force north to the west side of the ford. Canby himself was not in the vanguard led by a Lieutenant Colonel Roberts.

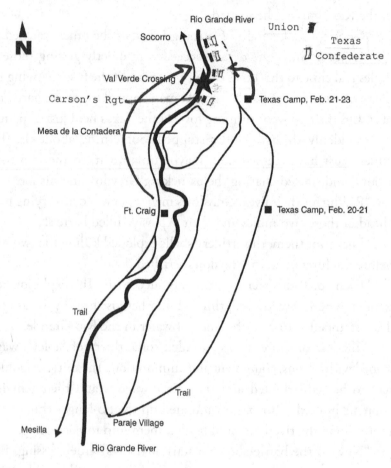

★ **Battle of Val Verde, February 22, 1862**

Rio Grande River

Socorro

Union

Texas
Confederate

Val Verde Crossing

Carson's Rgt

Texas Camp, Feb. 21-23

Mesa de la Contadera*

Ft. Craig

Texas Camp, Feb. 20-21

Trail

Trail

Mesilla

Paraje Village

Rio Grande River

One Inch = Approx. One Mile

*also spelled "Mesa del Contadero"

"Roberts' order of march was cavalry--four troops under Major Robert Duncan--followed by infantry and lots of artillery. That artillery was a six-howitzer battery commanded by a Captain McRae plus several other cannon firing 24-pound shells.

"A Texas battalion was already on the east bank and shootin' began as soon as Canby's vanguard arrived. The Union six-howitzer battery immediately crossed the river and began firing on the rebs facing them with good results. Union infantry surged across the icy river and charged the Texas line.

"Since my observation mission was complete I took my companies back across the river to the west side and reported to Colonel Canby. By midmorning on 21 February, me and my boys sat watching the fire fight raging across the river.

"Canby's vanguard seemed to be gaining the upper hand. I had the luxury of studying the Texans' positions from my seat on the west bank. But not fer long.

"About one o'clock in the afternoon I received orders from Colonel Canby to cross the river, which I immediately did. We formed on the right flank of the battle line and advanced as skirmishers toward the hills, alongside Duncan's cavalry.

"After advancing some 400 yards we ran into a large body--some 400 to 500--of enemy. They were charging diagonally across our front, trying to capture the 24-pound cannon on our right. That 24-pounder was advancing with us and causing lots of enemy casualties.

"As the enemy column approached within about 80 yards of us, a volley from our entire line let loose. That volley was repeated so effectively and so often that the rebs scattered in every direction.

"Canby's plan, and I thought it a good one, was to use McRae's six howitzers on the left as his pivot point." Carson marked the howitzers' position on the white buffalo hide with his charcoal.

"The rest of us, my regiment on the right, would pivot to our left like a trap door. Those constantly firing howitzers were the hinge about which we rotated toward the rebs.

"Almost at the same time our volleys stopped their charge on our side. A shell from our 24-pounder landed among 'em with fatal effect.

"Still moving forward, we cleared the woods ahead, placing us in an excellent position to rain enfilade fire on the entire reb formation on our left. That's when I received the surprise order from Canby to retreat and recross the river.

"Surprised or not, we followed orders. We crossed the river in good shape and returned to Fort Craig that evening.

"One of my company commanders was Captain Rafael Chacon who later bragged: 'We fought full of courage and almost in a frenzy, driving the enemy back through blood and fire…'

Chacon continued. "About the hour of sunset the retreat was sounded. I, with my mounted company, had driven far into the enemy's lines. For the moment I could not understand the signal to retreat for we considered that our charge upon the enemy's main cavalry had won the battle. I was so loathe to leave the field that my company was the last of our army to cross the river."

Carson paused to spit. "On the left side of the Union line, things weren't going as well as on the right. Canby's offensive over there faltered under a withering fire from the Texas batteries and repeated rebel charges. Lots of Union troops turned tail and ran back to the river. Many were shot down, trying to ford it.

"Canby's favorite horse, Old Chas, was shot out from under him, as were two other horses. Those Texans kept charging McRae's six-howitzer battery, the lynch pin of the Canby assault.

After bloody hand-to-hand fighting, the Texans captured McRae's battery. They reversed the six howitzers and began firing on the retreating, now panicky Union troops in the river.

"Faced with the loss of his best artillery unit *and* his favorite horse, Canby must have been mighty discouraged. Then, too, he saw lots of his troops trying to cross the river but being slaughtered by captured artillery—-formerly his--or by rebel shotguns.

"Canby came to a decision which he thought was the correct one under those circumstances.

"Like me at Adobe Walls, he decided to withdraw. In Canby's case, he ordered all of us back across the river. Once again on the western side, we were told to fall back to Fort Craig and resume the defensive.

"*Jest* like you at Adobe Walls, I didn't cotton to withdrawal at Valverde.

"Neither did my Valverde officers. I remember Captain Chacon shaking his head in disgust, saying 'We had penetrated the enemy zone and considered that our charge had won the battle!'

Carson suddenly stopped, accidentally dropping his empty tin cup in the process. "What's the point of all this, you're askin'?

"If nothing else, remember this," he gestured. "An order is an order even if you don't understand or agree with it. The commander giving it likely has a much different view of the battle before him than you do. He's probably thinking several steps ahead. Maybe, what happens tonight or tomorrow? Maybe…even next week?

"After Valverde, Colonel Canby still commanded a fighting force occupying an almost impregnable fortress which the rebs could not defeat. He had plenty of ammunition, provisions, medicine and fuel to fight until the next Spring if necessary.

"Sibley from his ambulance wagon declared he'd won the victory since his casualties were a few less than Canby's. He may have been so drunk he failed to remember that his troops had little food, warm uniforms, blankets, medicines or ammunition. Nor, I would add, did they respect their commander whom they nicknamed 'Ole Walking Whisky Keg.'

"Sibley's regiments originally were all cavalry. Now--without sufficient horses and mules—some had to became foot soldiers, facing winter weather, cold half-rations, worn down boots and no news from home.

"I ask each of you. Who was the better commander, Canby or Sibley?

"You can make your own judgments about my ordering our withdrawal from Adobe Walls. Probably you have already."

A hand shot up from the officers. It was Captain Fritz.

He stood up. "I can sympathize with your Colonel Canby. He'd just lost his favorite hoss shot from under him and seen that artillery battery overrun by the rebels.

"But, Colonel. Our situation at Adobe Walls was different. We still had our artillery," he nodded at Lieutenant Pettis, "and we were shootin' lots of Indians.

"Seems to me, we could have picked up and attacked toward the Comanche villages and done serious damage there."

Other officers were nodding in agreement with Fritz's words.

"We didn't even have many casualties at that point, if I 'member correctly."

Carson cleared his throat. "Don't *fergit*. The hostiles' strength was bigger than ours and was getting bigger by the minute. Lieutenant Pettis here estimated that there were maybe 3,000 warriors out there, repeatedly charging our few skirmishers and two howitzers around Adobe Walls.

"You're right. I didn't know our exact casualty numbers at that moment but suspected they were heavy. We were fully engaged, except for the 75 infantrymen and cavalry far to the rear, guarding our trains. Knowing where the trains *wuz,* the hostiles might have been attacking them at the same time."

Major McCleave stood and repeated what he'd said earlier. "There were more Indians fighting us than I'd even seen before, Colonel. And I pray to God that I never see that many again."

Captain Deus jumped to his feet. "I second that. And I'm obliged to say thank you, Colonel. We're all here and still wearing our hair. Thanks to you!"

Deus saluted and sat down.

Carson nodded. "Let's see the hands of who'd like to follow me back to Adobe Walls next winter to finish off those Comanches and Kiowas?"

He looked around him. No hands were raised. Instead, there were downcast, embarrassed looks.

"Well, I'll ask that question again once we're safely back at Fort Bascom.

"Gents, I thank you for your attention. Now, let's get some rest before we mount up early tomorrow morning and head *fer* home."

That night, Carson was awakened from sleep by a tug on his shoulder. He sat up. Captain Fritz squatted beside him.

"Sorry to disturb you, Colonel. But I couldn't wait 'til morning to speak to you.

"I want you to know that I meant no disrespect by my question, sir."

Carson squinted at the captain. "Of course not, son. I value your opinion. Now *git* under your blanket and rest up before dawn."

AFTER ACTION REPORT AND CRITIQUE

With a sigh, Carson began, after the officers call, to record the Adobe Walls fight for Brigadier General James H. Carleton, Commander of the Department of New Mexico. He wasn't to complete his report until 4 December at the Rio Blanco camp, about halfway to Fort Bascom.

Since Carson was illiterate he had to verbalize the report to another officer who transcribed it. These slowly developed, often illegible, reports sometimes contained errors of which Carson was unaware until questioned.

Carson's official report of the battle dispatched to General Carleton was the basis of the latter's General Order Number 4.

Neither Carson's autobiography, republished in 1966, nor his memoirs, republished in 1968, detail the battle at Adobe Walls. Appendix A is his official report to General Carleton in Santa Fe. It is a straightforward and detailed report, perhaps garnished with a few words (e.g., 'conjectured') by the officer (probably Lieutenant Edgar) penning the report for Carson.

That battle involved the largest number of Native Americans pitted against the U.S. Army. Not even the Battle of the Little Big Horn had more hostiles. The first battle of Adobe Walls is an important engagement not to be overlooked.

Carson's reticence is evident from a letter describing his return march. "I have arrived at this point (presumably Rita Creek) without any incident worthy of note."

What *was* worthy of note was Carson's decision to withdraw in the face of:

*the enemy strength, estimated outnumbering him 10:1,

*his force being surrounded by the enemy all afternoon at Adobe Walls,

*the exhausted physical condition of his men who had fought continually for thirty hours without adequate rest or rations,

*the scarcity of ammunition, particularly for the twin howitzers, as the battle developed,

*the pitiful condition of horses and mules, many of them wounded,

*the enemy's knowledge of and ability to envelop Carson's distant wagon trains which were protected by only seventy-five soldiers, and

*Carson's obligation to safeguard and evacuate his wounded.

If the howitzer fires had not been so effective, had their ammunition run out, had more of Carson's skirmishers been killed in the tall grass, the battle outcome might have been vastly different.

If fortune had not dealt kindly with Carson and his First New Mexico Cavalry, a massacre might have ensued. Had that happened, such an ending would have overshadowed the famous loss of Custer's Seventh Cavalry at the battle of the Little Big Horn twelve years later.

Carson didn't ponder long over the enemy's superior strength at Adobe Walls. Outnumbered ten to one, surrounded on a battlefield, and his main base some 250 miles away, his decision to withdraw was timely and correct.

WIN, LOSE OR DRAW?

Carson's report completed at the Rita Creek campsite commended his troops for their cool performance under intense fire at Adobe Walls.

A degree of optimism was evident when he reported the following. "I have taught these Indians a severe lesson, and hereafter they will be more cautious about how they engage a force of civilized troops."

Contrary to the above, the Mexican traders, who were present in the Comanche camps during the battle, told Lieutenant Pettis a different story years later. They claimed "had it not been for the two guns that shot twice...not a single white man would have escaped out of the valley of the Canadian."

Adobe Walls was the first known battle in which a Native American force caused the U.S. Army to withdraw from the battlefield.

General Orders Number 4, Department of New Mexico, dated 18 February 1865, tells a different and inaccurate story:

"Colonel Christopher Carson, First Cavalry, New Mexico Volunteers, with a command consisting of fourteen commissioned officers and three hundred twenty-one enlisted men and seventy-five Indians, Apaches and Utes, attacked a Kiowa village of about one hundred and fifty lodges, near the Adobe Fort, on the Canadian River, in Texas; and, after a severe fight, *compelled the Indians to retreat,* (italics added) with a loss of sixty killed and wounded. The village was then destroyed. The engagement commenced at 0830 hours and lasted without intermission until sunset."

The above official Army report was incorrect. The Kiowas and Comanches did not retreat. *Carson* did, and wisely so. In later years he conceded that his command had almost been wiped out.

Without the howitzers, he maintained "few (of his troops) would have been left alive...."

The Texas marker commemorating the First Battle of Adobe Walls is factual. It simply reads, in partr, "though Carson made a brilliant defense, the Indians won."

Many comparisons have been made between the battles of Adobe Walls and the Little Big Horn, which followed years later. At the Little Big Horn, Lieutenant Colonel George A. Custer's Seventh Cavalry was outnumbered and decimated by another combined force, this one Lakota, Northern Cheyenne and Arapaho.

A brief comparison of those two battles--one a withdrawal, the other, annihilation--is at Appendix B.

Appendix C outlines a similar sounding but vastly different battle taking place in the vicinity of Adobe Walls almost ten years later. The *Second* Battle of Adobe Walls had little in common with Carson's *First* Battle of Adobe Walls despite their common name.

BACK AT FORT BASCOM

10 December 1864:

Carson and his command returned to Fort Bascon, their starting point fifteen days after their near calamitous battle at Adobe Walls.

Instead of moving his troops into the decrepit barracks of the old fort, Carson quartered them outside. He chose a location where grass was abundant for the benefit of his recovering, badly conditioned mounts. One of Carson's sayings was to the effect "Without horses, you have no campaign, no army."

Brigadier General Carleton praised Carson's expedition and its results. "This brilliant affair adds another green leaf to the laurel wreath which you have won in the service to your country."

Other Carleton orders reduced Carson's command to zero strength by returning its various elements back to their original posts throughout the New Mexico Territory.

Another administrative task was Carson's returning the one hundred caliber .58 Springfield rifles issued him for the Scouts by the supply officer at Fort Union. Five rifles had been stolen by Scouts who immediately deserted with the rifles at the start of the expedition. Comanches captured three rifles from Scouts they had killed or wounded.

Carson did not hesitate to point out in a report to General Carleton the guilt of the New Mexico Superintendent of Indian Affairs, Michael Steck, and the Mexican (Comanchero) traders Steck allowed among the Kiowas and Comanches.

"On the day of the fight I destroyed a large amount of powder, lead, caps, etc. and I have no doubt that this and the very balls with which my men were killed and wounded were sold by these Mexicans not ten days before ...But I blame the Mexicans not half as much as I do Mr.

Steck, superintendent of Indian affairs, who gave them the pass to go and trade, he knowing that the Mexicans would take what they could sell best, which was powder lead and caps, and Mr. Steck should have known better than to give passes to these men to trade when every one knows that ammunition is all the Indians want at this time."

Carson was ready to return to Adobe Walls and finish the mission were he authorized a new force. For a return to Adobe Walls he wanted a total of 1,000 men including 700 mounted troopers, more animals plus two 6-pounder and two 12-pounder cannon. He also requested enough rations and supplies for four months.

TEXAS MARKER COMMEMORATING THE FIRST BATTLE OF ADOBE WALLS. IT READS IN PART "LARGEST INDIAN BATTLE IN CIVIL WAR. 15 MILES EAST AT RUINS OF BENT'S OLD FORT ON THE CANADIAN, 3000 COMANCHES AND KIOWA...MET 372 FEDERALS UNDER COL. KIT CARSON, FAMOUS SCOUT AND MOUNTAIN MAN. ALTHOUGH CARSON MADE A BRILLIANT DEFENSE, THE INDIANS WON." (Courtesy: Texas Historical Commission)

TAPS

Kit Carson.

In May 1865, General Carleton gave a new order to Colonel Carson. He was to establish a new camp along the Santa Fe Trail, between Fort Union, New Mexico, and Fort Dodge, Kansas in what is now the Oklahoma Panhandle. The camp's purpose was to improve the protection of settlers and their wagon trains heading west.

Camp Nichols would house three companies, contain a hospital, commissary, barracks and guardhouse. The construction began the next month but Carson was called away by Carleton before the task was completed.

In December, Carson became the commander of Fort Union, New Mexico. There he received the good news of his promotion to Brevet Brigadier General, New Mexico Volunteers.

The promotion notification and order did not arrive until later. It also cited the performance of Carson and his regiment at the battle of Valverde. On January 4, he repeated the necessary oath making him a Brigadier General.

Likely Kit Carson was the only general officer who had never been a lieutenant. Probably he was also the only illiterate general officer. That year he was transferred to Fort Garland, Colorado.

In early 1868, Carson traveled to Washington with his favorite Ute chiefs to petition for a permanent reservation for his friends.

It was physically a difficult trip. Not only did his physician, Doctor Henry Tilton, strongly advise him not to go, his wife Josefa was seven months pregnant.

After a successful negotiation, Carson and the Utes toured the city. They visited the War Department, saw President Andrew Jackson and the Washington Monument under construction. Carson even had a formal, uncomfortable-looking photograph made by the famed Civil War photographer, Mathew Brady.

Carson took time to consult with a prominent eastern physician, Doctor Lewis Sayre, hoping there was a miraculous cure for his worsening aortic aneurysm.

By the time Carson made a side trip to Boston, finally heading home, he was flat on his back, encased in robes and blankets. Josefa met him with a carriage near La Junta, Colorado on 11 April and took him home.

Two days later, Josefa gave birth to a baby girl whom Carson named Josefita after his wife.

Josefa felt somewhat better on 27 April, enough so she began brushing the hair of daughter Teresina.

Suddenly Josefa dropped the brush and called "Cristobal!" to her husband. He stumbled from his pallet of blankets in time to hold Josefa a moment before she died.

On the following 23 May, the mourning Carson's appetite suddenly revived. He asked Doctor Tilton for a big dinner of buffalo steak cooked in red *chiles* and a pot of coffee, just like old times.

Faithful Tilton acceded to his patient's requests. Later, sitting on the floor beside Carson in his buffalo robes, Tilton heard Carson's last words.

"Doctor, *compadre, adios.*"

Carson was buried beside his wife at Fort Lyon as an Army bugler played taps and the flag was half-staffed.

At Carson's request, he and Josefa were later reburied near their Taos, New Mexico home. At his death, Denver's *Rocky Mountain News* published the following:

"Over what an immense expanse of plains, of snow-clad sierra, of rivers, lakes and seas, has he cut the first paths? His guiding instinct was an innate chivalry. He had in him a personal courage which came forth when wanted, like lightening from a cloud."

Kiowa Chief Dohasan (Sierrito)

His name can be translated as Little Mountain, Little Bluff or Top of the Mountain. He was a member of the Kata clan or sept as well as belonging to the elite Kiowa warrior society, the Koitsenko. Dohasan gathered and led his warriors against the bluecoats at his overrun village, then forced eastward, against Carson's troops at Adobe Walls. Dohasan had his horse shot from under him while leading charges against the bluecoats. He alerted the Comanche chiefs down river of the Carson threat. Among his many honors was the "calendar keeper" of the tribe, responsible for the annual pictorals prepared on buffalo hides during the summer Sun Dance. His account, painted on buffalo hides, highlighted the period as a "muddy travel winter, the time the Kiowa repelled Kit Carson."

Not only did Chief Dohasan live through the battle at Adobe Walls, he was the principal chief of the Kiowas for an unusually long period of 33 years. He died in Oklahoma in 1866.

Lieutenant George H. Pettis

Carson's artillery commander and his gunners were responsible for the withering effective firepower of the two mountain howitzers. Pettis' battery decimated the ranks of charging warriors, allowing Carson's beleaguered troops to form an escape column in the midst of battle, successfully withdrawing back to the west.

Pettis was the chronicler of the expedition. His diary of the approach march and battle were published in 1908.

Among Pettis' stories were his 1867 conversations with two Mexican traders actually present while the battle raged. The traders were held prisoner in the larger Comanche village down river from Adobe Walls. According to them, the Indians suffered more casualties than Carson's estimate. The traders said nearly 100 warriors were killed that day and another 100-150 were wounded. This confirmed Pettis' opinion expressed to Carson and others on the day after the battle that Carson's estimate of sixty killed and wounded was low.

The Indians claimed that, were it not for the two howitzers ("guns that shot twice"), not a single white man would have escaped from the valley of the Canadian that day.

Later Pettis was promoted to Captain in the California Volunteers. In 1868 he moved to Rhode Island from Oklahoma. There he served as a member of the state house of representatives from 1876-1877. In 1899

Pettis became the resident surveyor of the village of Pawtuxet where he died in 1901.

Brigadier General James Henry Carleton

Commander of the Department of New Mexico from 1862 to 1868, Carleton relied on Carson's expertise, judgment and sure performance throughout his career. Like Carson, he had no Military Academy training but was commissioned as a lieutenant during the Aroostock War. His highest rank was Brevet Major General of New Mexico Volunteers. Carleton later accepted the permanent rank of Lieutenant Colonel in the 4th U.S. Cavalry. He died while serving in San Antonio, Texas, in January 1873.

Comanche Chief Ten Bears

Ten Bears (or Paruasemena) was principal chief of the Yamparika sept of the Comanches from 1860 to 1872. He led his warriors against Carson's troops at Adobe Walls. His son, Red Sleeves, was killed that afternoon. As a result of a Lakota raid in which his family was killed, Ten Bears was raised an orphan. Later he fought alongside the Cheyenne against Lieutenant Colonel George A. Custer when the latter led a merciless surprise attack against the peaceful village of Black Kettle. Ten Bears also accompanied two delegations of Indian leaders to Washington to present their case for Indian equity. At one conference, Chief Ten Bears deplored the Texans presence:

"If the Texans had kept out of my country, there might have been peace. But that which you say we must live in is too small. The Texans have taken away the places where the grass grew the thickest and the timber was best.

Had we kept that we might have done the things you asked. But it is too late. The whites have the country which we loved and we wish only to wander on the prairie 'til we die."

Chief Ten Bears died in 1872 and is buried at Fort Sill, Oklahoma.

APPENDIX A: OFFICIAL REPORT OF THE BATTLE OF ADOBE WALLS

The Kiowa-Comanche Expedition

Headquarters Kiowa and Comanche Expedition, Camp on the Rio Blanco, 100 Miles east of Fort Bascom, Dec. 4, 1864.

Captain: I have the honor to submit for the information of the general commanding the following report of my operations against the Kiowa and Comanche Indians:

I arrived at Fort Bascom, N.M., on the tenth ultimo, with seventy-five Ute and Apache Indians. At this place I found all the companies composing the expedition in readiness to move at any moment. I left Fort Bascom on the 12th ultimo with the following force, viz., Captain Fritz's Company (B First Cavalry, California Volunteers), 30 men; Lieutenant Heath, with a detachment of Company K, First Cavalry, California Volunteers, 38 men; Captain Deus' Company (M, First Cavalry, New Mexico Volunteers), Lieutenant Bishop and 69 men; Captain Berney's Company (D, First New Mexico Volunteers), 39 men; Lieutenant Edmiston, with 58 men of Company A, First Veteran Infantry, California Volunteers, and Lieutenant Pettis, with 27 men of Company K, First Infantry, California Volunteers, and two mountain howitzers. The infantry force was commanded by Lieut. Col. F.P. Abreu, First Infantry, New Mexico Volunteers, and the cavalry by Major William McCleave, First Cavalry California Volunteers. This force was accompanied by seventy-five Ute and Apache Indians, in charge of Lieut. Charles Haberkorn, First Cavalry, New Mexico Volunteers, whom I took with me for that purpose. Lieutenant J.C. Edgar accompanied me as act'g assistant adjutant general of the expedition. Lieut. B. Taylor, First U.S. Infantry, as acting assistant quartermaster and acting commissary of subsistence, and Asst. Surg. George S. Courtright, U.S. Volunteers, as surgeon to my command. Total, 14 officers and 321 enlisted men, and 75 Indians. (Note: Carson seems to have inadvertently omitted Captain Witham's company, named in general orders, counting 60 men, which would bring his enlisted total to 321.) This force was subsisted to include December 31, 1864. I deemed it proper to take wagons as transportation as far as a point known as the Adobe fort, about 200 miles east of Fort Bascom, on the Canadian river, at which point I intended to form a depot and operate with pack mules. I considered that the number of pack saddles at my disposal (100) was insufficient to transport the necessary supply of subsistence to take me to the place where I expected to find an Indian encampment. Traveled by easy stages on a practicable wagon road along the north bank of the Canadian river, having to lay over for one day on two occasions on account of snowstorms. On the 24th ultimo, while encamped on a creek known as the Arroya de la Mula, about thirty miles west of the Adobe fort, I dispatched two Indian spies with instructions to proceed a distance down the Canadian, and return the same evening if they saw any fresh signs of Indians. They returned about one hour after sundown, and gave me information from which I concluded that there was a camp of hostile Kiowa and Comanche Indians in my vicinity. I immediately gave orders to have all the wagons loaded and left in charge of Lieutenant Colonel Abreu with the infantry and dismounted cavalry force, and I moved forward with my entire mounted force and Lieutenant Pettis' howitzers. I marched about fifteen miles that night and again encamped and sent my spies ahead. They returned about two hours before daybreak, when I immediately took the saddle and continued my march down the river.

About one hour after daybreak on the 25th ultimo I discovered a party of Indians on the opposite bank of the river who were calling to me to cross over. I ordered Major McCreave with Captain Deus' company to cross over and pursue them, and I continued my march along the river. Soon after I discovered an Indian encampment about five miles in advance. I immediately directed Captain Fritz to advance with his company and act in conjunction with Major McCreave, who was on the opposite side of the river with Captain Deus' company. On hearing the report of small arms in front, I concluded that a fight had commenced and I directed Lieutenant Heath, with his detachment, to advance, and I followed as fast as possible with the artillery and Captains Witham's and Birney's companies. The Indians abandoned their camp of about 150 lodges, but hotly contested the ground between there and the Adobe fort, a distance of about four miles. At this point they took a position and made a stand. They made several severe charges on Major McCleave's command before my arrival with the artillery and the other companies, but were gallantly repulsed. On my arrival on the ground I ordered the artillery to take a position, and the engagement ceased for a short time. Finding it impossible due to the broken down condition of my cavalry horses, to capture any more of the stock which the Indians had in their possession, I gave orders to unsaddle, and the men to have breakfast, it being my intention to return and destroy the Indian village through which I had passed. On looking through my glass I discovered a large force of Indians advancing from another village about three miles east of Adobe fort. In this village there were at least 350 lodges. I immediately ordered the command to saddle and the companies to take position. In a short time I found myself surrounded by at least 1,000 Indian warriors mounted on first class horses. They repeatedly charged my command from different points, but were invariably repulsed with great loss. The two mounted howitzers, under Lieutenant Pettis, did good service, and finally drove the Indians out of range. The Indians still remained in my vicinity and I conjectured that it was their opinion to keep me in my position at the Adobe fort if possible until night, that they might have an opportunity to carry off their lodges and provisions from their village, also some stock they had left behind in their retreat. I therefore determined to return to the village and destroy it. I now gave orders for Captain Fritz to protect my right flank, dismounted and deployed as skirmishers; Captain Witham's and a part of Captain

Deus' company on the left flank, and Captain Birney's and Lieutenant Heath's detachment, and a part of Captain Deus' company in the same manner to protect the rear. In this manner I commenced my march on the village. The Indians, seeing my object, again advanced, with the evident intention of saving their village and property if possible.. The Indians charged so repeatedly and with such desperation that for some time I had serious doubts for the safety of my rear, but the coolness with which they were received by Captain Birney's command, and the steady and constant fire poured into them, caused them to retire on every occasion with great slaughter.

The Indians now finding it impossible to impede my march by their repeated charges, set fire to the valley in my rear, which was composed of long grass and weeds, and the wind being favorable it burned with great fury and caused my rear to close up double quick. I immediately saw their object and had the valley fired to my front to facilitate my march. I then retired to a piece of elevated ground on my right flank upon which the grass was short, and upon which I knew I was out of danger from the fire. Here the Indians again advanced under cover of the fire and smoke which raged with great fury, but my artillery being in position they were again repulsed with great slaughter. The fighting was constantly kept up in rear until I arrived within 500 yards of the Indian village, when the Indians made a charge forward for the purpose of rescuing a part of their property. However, a few shells from my howitzers, which were immediately put in position, drove them yelling from the ground, and the entire village and stores were in my possession. I then proceeded to destroy the village and stores, amounting to about 150 lodges of the best manufacture, a large amount of dried meat, berries, buffalo robes, powder, cooking utensils, etc., also a buggy and spring wagon, the property of Sierrito, or Little Mountain, the Kiowa chief of the Indians which I engaged. The principal number were Kiowas with a small number of Comanches, Apaches and Arapahoes, all of which were armed with rifles, and I must say they acted with more daring and bravery than I have ever before witnessed. The engagement commenced about 8:30 a.m., and lasted I may say without intermission until sunset, during which time I had 2 soldiers killed and 10 wounded, and 1

Indian killed and 5 wounded, and a large number of horses wounded (see the inclosed list). It is impossible for me to form a correct estimate of the enemy's loss, but from the number which I saw fall from their horses during the engagement I cannot call it less than 60 in killed and wounded. I flatter myself that I have taught these Indians a severe lesson, and that hereafter they will be more cautious about how they engage a force of civilized troops. The officers and men engaged acted with the utmost coolness during the fight and my entire command showed a promptitude in carrying out my orders on all occasions.

I take pleasure in bringing to your notice the names of the following officers whose conduct during the fight deserves the highest praise: they are Major McCleave, Captain Fritz, and Lieut. Heath, First Cavalry, California Volunteers; Captains Deus and Birney, First Cavalry, New Mexico Volunteers. Lieutenant Pettis' howitzers were well served and did remarkable good service. Lieut. J.C. Edgar, First Cavalry, New Mexico Volunteers, acting assistant adjutant general of expedition, was remarkable for his coolness and bravery during the engagement. I am indebted to Assistant Surgeon Courtright, U.S. Volunteers, for his prompt attention to the wounded of my command. The Ute and Apache Indians acted bravely during the day.

The Indians seeing their village in flames fled to the hills and gave me no further annoyance. I regret very much that the poor condition of my horses did not permit me to follow them and secure a large amount of stock which they had in their possession, also another large village which I could observe through my glass farther down the river. The company commanders now reported to me their ammunition was nearly expended. I deemed it prudent to return and join my wagons, which I directed to follow me slowly. About 8:30 p.m. I came upon Colonel Abreu's command encamped with the entire train on a creek about ten miles west of the Adobe fort. Here I also encamped for the night. In the morning I moved my entire command about 500 yards for the purpose of procuring better grass for my animals. I now decided that owing to the broken-down condition of my cavalry horses and transportation and the Indians having fled in all directions with their stock that it was impossible for me to chastise them further at present. Therefore, on the morning of the 27th ultimo, I broke camp and commenced my return trip. I have traveled by easy marches in order that I may take all my animals to the fort if possible, and I have arrived at this point without incident worthy of note. I shall continue to travel slowly to Fort Bascom, where I expect to arrive about the 10th instant, and I will await there for further instructions from the general commanding.

I am, captain, very respectfully, your obedient servant,

C. CARSON

Colonel First Cavalry, New Mexico Vols., Comdg.

Captain Benjamin C. Cutler

Asst. Adjt. Gen., Dept. of New Mexico, Santa Fe, N. Mex.

APPENDIX B: COMPARING CARSON AND CUSTER

"A bold operation is one in which success is not a certainty but which, in case of failure, leaves one with sufficient forces in hand to cope with whatever situation may arise. A gamble, on the other hand, is an operation which can lead either to victory or to complete destruction of one's force. Erwin Rommel

THEIR MISSIONS:

Carson: Punish the Kiowa and Comanche by destroying winter villages and all possessions. Find and defeat enemy resistance.

Custer: Force the Lakota and Cheyenne warriors to surrender and return to their reservations by capturing their villages, women, children and elderly. Find and defeat enemy resistance.

Comment: Carson's mission was partially completed. Only the Kiowa village was destroyed not the numerous down river camps of the Comanche. Although Custer inflicted heavy casualties upon Cheyenne, Arapaho and Lakota warriors, none surrendered.

THEIR BACKGROUNDS:

Carson lacked the formal training Custer enjoyed as a cadet at the Military Academy where he was a member of the class of 1862. During his time at West Point, Custer accumulated a record 726 demerits, graduating number 34 out of 34. If his academic record was unimpressive, his extracurricular was its equal: he contracted gonorrhea while at the Academy.

One commonality: both Carson and Custer were fluent in sign language.

Carson was married three times while Custer was married once in 1861. Custer's wife, Libbie, frequently went campaigning with her husband. There was a later reported relationship between Custer and a Cheyenne "exceedingly comely squaw." (his words) named Spring Grass. Eventually Spring Grass gave birth to two children, which may or may not have been Custer's.

The majority of Carson's Civil War combat was at the battle of Valverde where he successfully commanded a New Mexico Volunteer regiment. Custer had a distinguished Civil War record serving under Generals McClellan, Pleasonton, and Sheridan. His bravery and dash were as unmistakable as his penchant for non-regulation uniforms, like buckskins and red scarves. One New York paper dubbed Custer "the boy General with his flowing yellow curls." Indeed Custer was the youngest general (holding the temporary rank or brevet of Brigadier General) in the U.S. Army at the early age of 23.

In contrast, Kit Carson was neither dashing nor fastidious in uniform. Most of his combat experience was with Indians, whose hit, run and scatter habits he knew well. Before the Indians, Custer employed the tactics he learned at West Point and polished in combat during the Civil War. His approach to Indian warfare was to capture noncombatants (women, children, and the elderly) and hold them hostage until their warrior relatives surrendered.

Among the men and officers of the Seventh Cavalry, Custer's leadership was often in question. His officers enjoyed good rations while his men ate old bread and maggoty beef. Once Custer, without permission, left his command for a prolonged visit with his family in Kansas. He was court-martialed on two charges: AWOL and for having several of his own soldiers shot for desertion without trial. The court's wrist-slap sentence was Custer's suspension from duty without pay for one year.

That suspension later was reduced by several months and Custer returned to duty. To redeem and renew his fame, he led a surprise attack on a peaceful Cheyenne winter encampment on the Washita River in what is now western Oklahoma in 1868. He claimed 150 Indians were killed of a village population of about 250 Cheyenne.

Custer's intelligence was criminally wrong: this Cheyenne clan on the Washita was at peace. Their chief, Black Kettle, displayed a white flag near his lodge to announce their peaceful intentions. Black Kettle and his wife were shot down in front of their tepee. Many women and children were similarly slain. Custer's rumored Cheyenne consort, Spring Grass, was taken hostage during this massacre.

In the ensuing battle with other Indians joining the Cheyenne in defense of their homes and families, Custer was guilty of an unpardonable command sin. He left a portion of his force on the battlefield that night without waiting its return from a mission or ascertaining its status. Major Joel Elliott, Custer's second-in-command, and seventeen troopers were found in a small defensive circle. When Custer returned to the Washita *two weeks later.* He found Elliott and all his men killed, their bodies mutilated.

PERSONNEL STRENGTHS:

Adobe Walls*(Carson)   Little Big Horn**(Custer)

US: 350 Enemy:2000/3000   US: 647 Enemy:900/2500

---

* Carson's "Official Report on the Battle of Adobe Walls"
** Wikipedia, "Battle of the Little Bighorn"

Comment: Carson's strength was 17.5% of Pettis' initial estimate of 2000 warriors or 11.6% of his later estimate of 3000. Custer's strength was 71.8% of the low estimate of 900 warriors or 25.8% of the high estimate of 2500.

Custer saw through his binoculars a huge, sprawling Indian village fifteen miles ahead. Due to this observation, he estimated his enemy at 2000 warriors. He must have realized that his total force of less than 700 troopers would be vastly outnumbered. Boasting earlier, he claimed "There are not enough Indians in the world to defeat the Seventh Cavalry."

CASUALTIES:

Adobe Walls*(Carson)	Little Big Horn**(Custer)
US: rate (18/350)=5%	US: rate (323/647)=49.9%
Enemy: (60/2000)= 3%	Enemy: (296/900)=32.8%
Enemy: (60/3000)= 2%	Enemy: (296/2500)=11.8%

Comment: Carson's casualty rate was much lower than Custer's. Custer inflicted much higher casualties upon the enemy than did Carson.

CRITIQUE:

Carson:

Hearing taunts across the river from three Kiowa "pickets", Carson divided his command. He ordered Major McCleave, one California company, one New Mexico detachment and the Indian Scouts to cross the river, pursue and engage the three hostiles. This left the rest of his force (including the twin howitzers) at risk on the same side of the river as the Kiowa encampment where the majority of its warriors could be presumed to have been alerted.

He failed to use his Scouts to best advantage. They might have provided additional intelligence about strength and locations of the Comanche villages further down river from the Adobe Walls.

Custer:

Depending on U.S. Indian Agencies for his initial intelligence about the size of the enemy, Custer underestimated his enemy's strength. By releasing his Crow scouts before the engagement, he denied himself their valuable intelligence collection capabilities.

Based on faulty information, he severely divided his force, diminishing its combat capability. Of the twelve companies originally under Custer, he detached three to Major Reno and three to Captain Benteen. Of the five companies under his direct control, Custer further delegated two to Captain Yates. The twelfth company was assigned to protect the pack train.

Custer turned down offered reinforcements of two battalions of the 2d Cavalry. He also declined two available Gatling guns (an early heavy machine gun) thus depriving his command of a valuable, although cumbersome, large caliber crew-served weapon. Carson handily employed his two howitzers. Custer refused two lethal heavy weapons.

The Seventh Cavalry's small arms were not the equal of those of most of the Lakota and Cheyenne. Many warriors carried repeating carbines or rifles. Custers' men were armed with single shot breech-loading Springfield carbines and rifles.

Custer concentrated on taking women, children, and elderly noncombatants prisoner, hoping to subdue--not necessarily fight--their warriors.

Custer's ambition, flamboyant reputation and appetite for risk may have lessened his caution about fighting Native Americans. The entirety of Custer's group of some 210 men were killed after about twenty minutes of intense combat with the Cheyenne and Lakota.

In an interview with the *New York Herald*, President U.S. Grant said, "I regard Custer's Massacre as a sacrifice of troops brought on by Custer himself, that was wholly unnecessary-—wholly unnecessary."

APPENDIX C: THE SECOND BATTLE OF ADOBE WALLS*

Although sounding alike, the first and second battles of Adobe Walls had little in common. Their commonality was their free-ranging, buffalo-dependent Plains Indian enemy. The Native Americans naturally viewed settlers and pioneers--especially buffalo hunters--as encroachments and dangers to their sustenance and way of life.

Shortly before the second battle on 27 June 1874, four hunters had been killed by Indians in different Panhandle locales. Those killings precipitated a gathering of a number of buffalo hunters at the Adobe Walls settlement.

The *second* battle was fought some ten years after the first. It happened at a location about a mile away from the Adobe Walls ruins behind which Carson and his cavalry and artillery fought for their lives on 25 November 1864.

At the Second Battle of Adobe Walls, groups representing several tribes (Comanche, Kiowa, Cheyenne) attacked and besieged a group of commercial buffalo hunters.

The initial strength of the hunters was twenty-eight. Estimates of the attacking Indians range from 250 to 1500 warriors.

The new settlement near the old Adobe Walls fort contained several buildings: a Leonard&Meyers store and corral, O'Keefe's blacksmith shop, the bar/saloon of James Hanarahan and a second store. A Mr.

---

* Wikipedia, "Second Battle of Adobe Walls"

Langston operated the latter, purchasing and trading buffalo hides with the 200-300 hunters roaming the Panhandle high plains of Texas.

Among those Americans present at the settlement on 25 June were the famous "Bat" Masterson, saloonkeeper Hanrahan, "Billy" Dixon and one woman, the wife of cook William Olds.

At 0200 hours on 27 June, a loud report (like that of a rifle) awakened everyone in the settlement. The saloonkeeper, Hanrahan, may have fired the shot himself.

As if on cue, Comanche and Kiowa mounted warriors, estimated at more than 700, attacked the settlement at dawn. One of the principal chiefs leading the attack was the famous Quanah Parker whose mother, Cynthia Ann Parker, had been kidnapped by the Comanches years before.

Luckily for the hunters, all were awake due to the loud noise heard at 0200 hours. Unluckly for the hunters, the Indians were soon hammering on their doors with rifle butts. The hunters had to resort to pistols and short range lever action rifles to beat away the warriors.

The hunters' weapon of choice was the large caliber, long range rifle with which they hunted buffalo. Initially the Indians were too close for the deadly buffalo guns to be effectively employed.

Eventually nine of the big guns were firing from Hanrahan's saloon where Masterson and Dixon had taken refuge. Eleven hunters operated their buffalo rifles from the Leonard&Meyers store. Another seven or eight were firing from Langston's buffalo hide store.

By noon, the Indians had pulled back, firing sporadically at the settlement. By 1400 hours they wisely retreated out of range of the buffalo hunters' big rifles. That day three hunters were killed by Indian fire.

The total number of Indians killed that first day is unknown since their habit was to immediately retrieve the body of any slain warrior. Nonetheless, fifteen warrior bodies were discovered the first day. The bodies were too close to the buildings to be safely retrieved by their comrades.

Day two of the siege saw the hunters drag off many of the dead horses around the settlement because of their smell. Reinforcements were received and messengers dispatched to Dodge City, Kansas, for more support. Two other hunters volunteered to pass the warning to other hunter camps in the area.

On third day of the siege fifteen warriors rode up a bluff over a mile away from the settlement. "Billy" Dixon borrowed a big rifle from Hanrahan and made the most famous rifle shot in Western history.

From a range of nearly one mile, Dixon was able to kill one of the mounted warriors on the far bluff. Discouraged by Dixon's amazing marksmanship, the others rode away.

More reinforcements arrived at the settlement on days three, four and five, increasing the settlement strength to about 100.

During the battle Comanche chieftain Quanah Parker was wounded. This was an extremely bad omen for the attackers. One estimate was that nearly 30 warriors had been killed at the Second Battle of Adobe Walls.

In August a cavalry troop arrived at the settlement where American strength had dwindled since the battle to about a dozen men. The next day the cavalry and remaining hunters abandoned the settlement. Later, the Indians burned down the buildings where they had been repulsed and the great chief Quanah Parker wounded.

"Billy" William Dixon was eventually buried nearby, not far from the spot where he made his famous rifle shot. That amazing feat of marksmanship evidently discouraged further Indian charges. Later measurements indicated the range of that single, fatal rifle shot was 1,538 yards or nine tenths of a mile.

THE EXCELLENT HISTORICAL REFERENCES TO WHICH THE AUTHOR IS INDEBTED

Carson, Kit, "Kit Carson's Autobiography," editor, M.M. Quaife, Lincoln,NE: University of Nebraska Press, 1966.

Carter, H.L., "Dear Old Kit", The Historical Christopher Carson, and New Edition of the Carson Memoirs," Norman, OK: University of Oklahoma Press, 1968.

Fehrenbach, T.R., "Comanches: The History of a People," New York, NY: Random House, 1974.

Fehrenbach, T.R. "Comanches: The Destruction of a People," Bridgewater, NJ: Baker and Taylor, 1996.

Gwynne, S.C., "Empire of the Southern Moon," New York, NY: Scribner, 2010.

Kavanagh, T.W., "The Comanches: A History, 1706-1875," Lincoln, NE: University of Nebraska Press, 1996.

Lynn, A.R., "Kit Carson and the First Battle of Adobe Walls," Lubbock, TX: Texas Tech Press, 2014.

Morgan, Robert, "Lions of the West," New York, NY: Workman Publishing Co., 2011.

O'Reilly, Bill, "Legends and Lies," New York, NY: Henry Holt and Company, 2015.

Pettis, G. H., "Kit Carson's Fight with the Comanche and Kiowa Indians," Santa Fe, NM: The New Mexican Printing Company, 1908.

Sabin, Edwin L., "Kit Carson Days, 1809-1868," vol. II, Lincoln, NE: University of Nebraska Press, 1995.

Sides, Hampton, "Blood and Thunder," New York, NY: Doubleday, 2006.

Sullivan, Roy, "The Civil War in Texas and the Southwest," Bloomington, IN: AuthorHouse, 2007.

Taylor, John, "Bloody Valverde," Albuquerque, NM: University of New Mexico Press, 1995.

Wikipedia

Printed in the United States
by Bookmasters

Printed in the United States
By Bookmasters